A Spot of Summer

ANJ Press

Pittsburgh

A SPOT OF SUMMER
ANJ Press, First edition. AUGUST 2025.
Copyright © 2025 Amelia Addler.
Written by Amelia Addler.

Cover design by Lori Jackson
https://www.lorijacksondesign.com/

Maps by MistyBeee

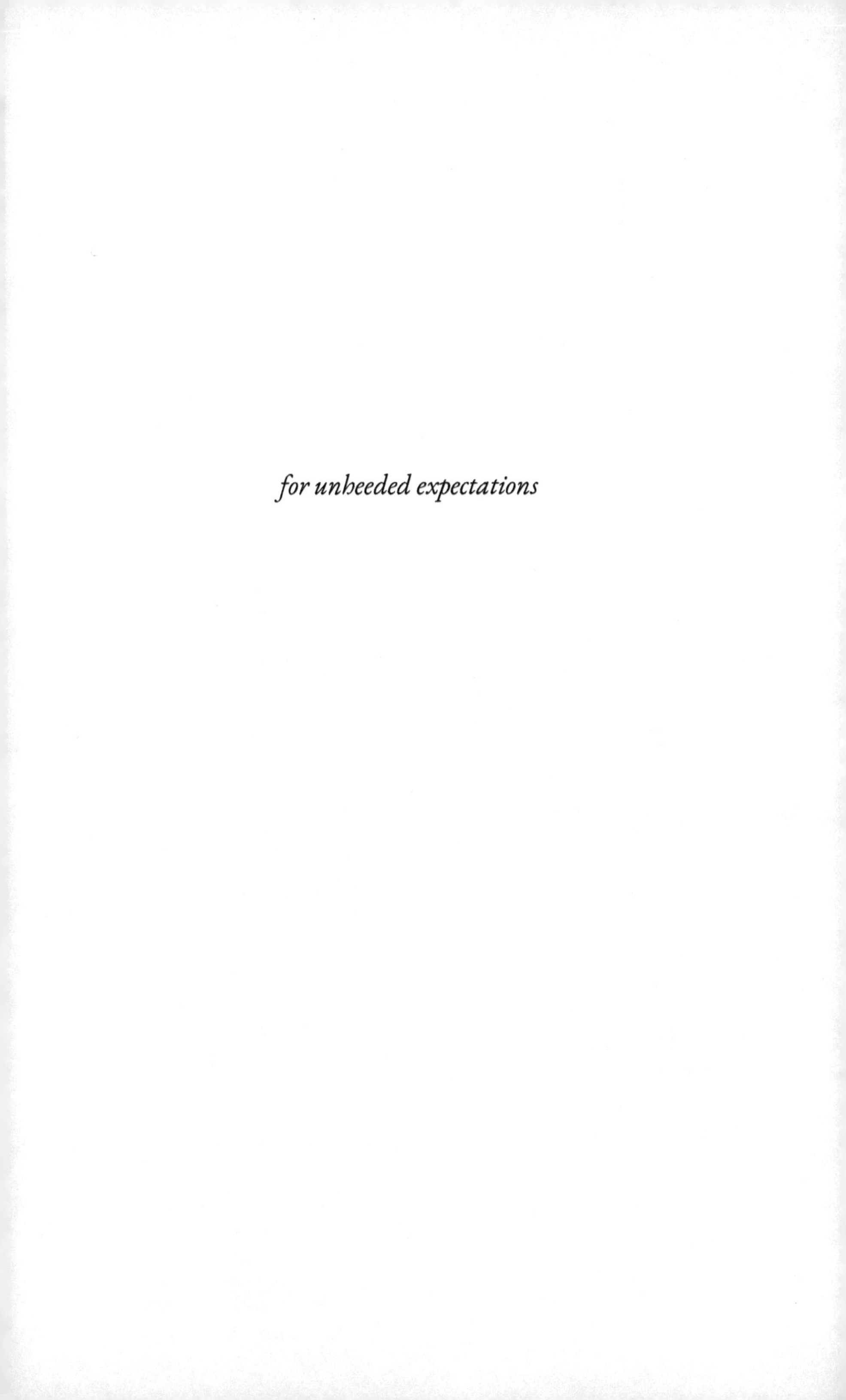

for unheeded expectations

Recap and Introduction to
A Spot of Summer

Growing up, Mia Westwood didn't know much about Hollywood. Her parents had once had careers as actors, but it was a blip in the past. It wasn't something that affected their family – until her mom, Holly Seville, spectacularly relaunched her career as a leading lady.

Success was a double-edged sword. Holly found happiness, but the craziness of fame contributed to Mia's parents getting divorced. Her dad, Russell Westwood, stepped away from acting and focused his attention on San Juan Island. Between meeting Sheila, the love of his life, and rehabilitating Lottie the orca, his days became busy and filled with joy.

After Mia's mom convinced her to try acting, she starred in her first movie – a superhero blockbuster and total dud.

Not giving up, Mia made another movie, this time starring alongside her mom. After filming wrapped, Mia decided to hide out at her dad's house for the summer. Her plan was to wait for the movie's release in the peace and quiet of San Juan Island.

Except the island had other plans, particularly when it comes to the handsome and mysterious Jacob Kowalski...

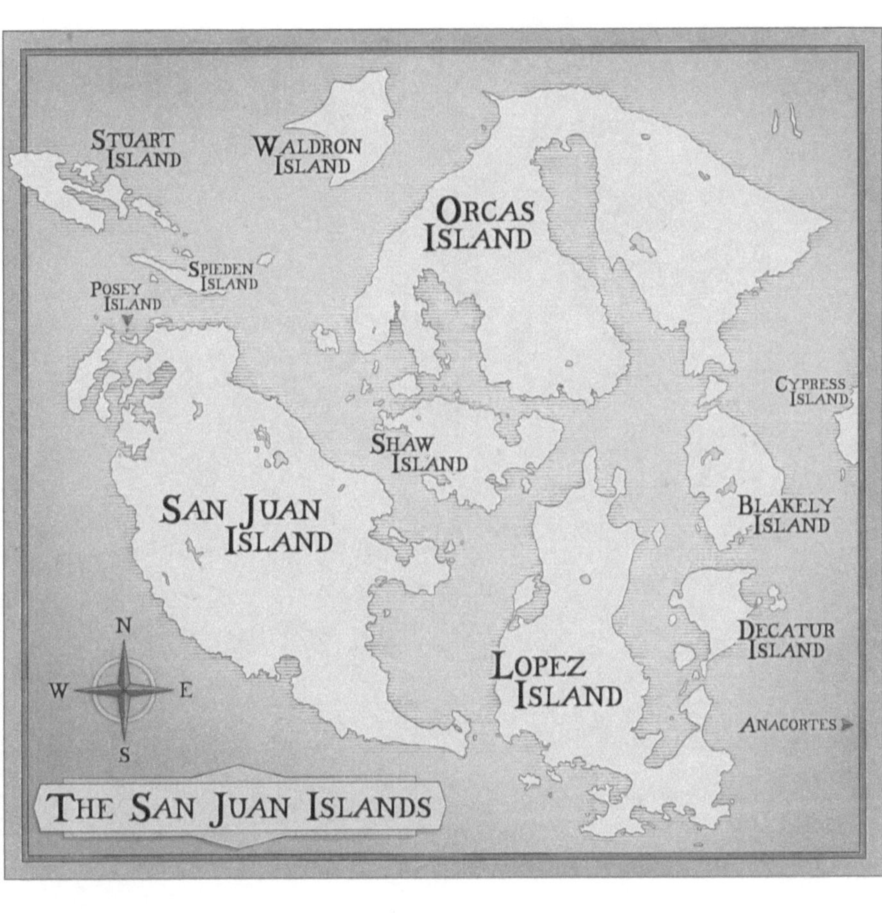

STUART ISLAND
WALDRON ISLAND
ORCAS ISLAND
SPIEDEN ISLAND
POSEY ISLAND
CYPRESS ISLAND
SHAW ISLAND
SAN JUAN ISLAND
BLAKELY ISLAND
DECATUR ISLAND
LOPEZ ISLAND
ANACORTES
N
W E
S
THE SAN JUAN ISLANDS

One

Forty-two days until the movie premiere. Forty-one nights watching the ceiling fan spin in the darkness, the promise of stars and sea just beyond her window.

Enough of that, though. It was a new day, and she had mountains to climb – literally and figuratively.

This movie could launch Mia's acting career. Her mom was convinced it would.

"Your career," her mom insisted, "is a carefully guided ship."

Carefully guided seemed a misnomer, and launches were anything but careful. Launches were violent! A ship with a combustion engine meant gasoline and explosions. Her career might take off, but who was to say the old thing wouldn't blast to pieces and scatter over the horizon?

Mia wasn't sure what she had was even considered a career. A handful of commercials, a stint as a juror in a true crime documentary, and a face-planting flop in a superhero movie.

Not impressive.

A drop of sweat sprouted from her temple and slid off her jaw. This hike was a lot harder than she'd expected. They called it Young Hill. It was more like Young Mountain.

She sucked in a breath. The island's crisp air fused with a warm smell from her hiking pack – chicken, onions, sauce. The sub she'd gotten for a snack.

The internet said she was supposed to pack nuts and granola for a hike, but she'd been in a hurry that morning. Mia had meant to get out on the trail early, but one thing had led to another, and then to the sub shop. The enchanting smell was the only thing keeping her going on this nightmare.

Up was the only way through. That was another one of her mom's famous lines. "When you're in a hole, the only way out is up."

Mia was in a hole all right, and she had to go up to find a spot where she could sit and eat her sub. She took a swig of water and kept walking.

Her role as Starlight Echo had won an award for "Cringiest Superhero of All Time," something strangers loved to shout at her when they spotted her in public. It had been a few weeks since that had happened, though. Moving to San Juan Island to hide out with her dad had helped.

Her dad hadn't even wanted a career, yet he'd ended up with one. The mysterious Russell Westwood delighted audiences with his surprising film choices and disappearances into eccentric characters.

Except he wasn't mysterious. Not to her. He'd spent years dragging their family to roadside attractions, making them wait until he read every educational placard in detail. He started conversations with strangers and invited people to join their table at restaurants. He wore bad hats and told even worse jokes. He was a dad.

Her mom's career was far more intentional. She reinvented herself as Holly Seville, a gorgeous middle-aged powerhouse who never took *no* for an answer. Of course she believed Mia's career would take off like a rocket ship – hers had.

Mia stopped, a stitch piercing her side. The cool air lit her lungs ablaze, and both of her legs shook as she stood.

Maybe Mia was a ship, too, but not the kind her mom imagined. She was an old, wooden boat, with creaking boards and a dingy sail blown ragged at the edges. Her movement wasn't plotted by engineers. She rode the wind with a hand-drawn map and gusts of naïve hope.

How could she not be at the top of this hill yet? She pulled out the hiking book and stared at the map, searching for wherever she must've made a wrong turn.

It looked right, as far as she could tell. The book said there would be amazing views at the top. A place for solitude, hopefully, and peace.

She tossed the book into her backpack and zipped it shut. Back on her shoulders, the straps dug into her skin, cold with sweat. Maybe it wasn't only her hiking boots that she should've broken in. Maybe this new, top-of-the-line hiking pack could've used some wearing down.

Too late now. She was doing this hike, armed with only the hiking book and advice from online strangers.

Mia heaved herself forward, her boots crunching on gravel, step after step. The trail's incline leveled out and she left the smell of pine needles behind. Evergreens framed the trail, thinning out, opening to a panorama of blue water and rolling hills.

"Finally," she whispered. She relaxed her shoulders and walked until she reached an overlook, sea and land stretching to the horizon. White clouds hung in the sky, and dots of boats moved below in slow motion below.

The wind filled her ears, waxing and waning. She snapped a picture, then pulled out the sub.

The cheese had hardened, but the bread was still crispy. Peace at last.

For a moment, the wind died down. In the quiet, the wails of an injured animal whispered over the hill.

Mia tilted her head. What animals were even up here? Deer? A lost dog?

She sighed, re-wrapping her sub and putting it in her pack. She stood, following the sound, her footsteps light on the bald rock face of the mountain. She came upon a patch of trees and spotted a woman hunched over, sobbing into her hands.

Whoops. Not an injured animal. At least not one she could help. She took three swift steps backward and something rolled under her shoe. A branch, cracking under her weight, at the same moment the weak muscles of her legs gave out.

She hit the ground with a thud and threw out her arms, trying to stop the tumble, but it was no use. Mia spun, cascading down the hill until she thudded abruptly into the trunk of a red-barked madrona tree.

She let out a groan. Was it really over? Or had she fallen off the mountainside?

A woman's voice floated in. "Are you okay?"

Mia struggled to her feet, pain flashing at her ankle like flames of a fire. She took a stumbling step forward. "Yes, I'm fine."

"You don't look fine."

Mia squinted into the sun – was that Bailey Jo Collins? *The* Bailey Jo Collins?

"Just a little spill." Mia raised a hand to her face, wiping away dirt. She kept wiping, taking a moment to realize her hands were caked with grit and dust, too.

Bailey Jo pointed at her head. "You're bleeding."

Mia touched a hand to her forehead and winced. "Ha, yeah, well, you should see the other guy."

"What other guy? Did someone push you?"

Mia sighed. "No, I was joking. I tripped."

Bailey Jo tilted her head. Her eyes were red and small. Her cheeks were splotched with color. "You look familiar."

"I'm Mia Westwood." She bent down and rubbed her ankle. The pain was less intense, but hadn't completely gone away. It felt creaky and uneasy, like the boards of her ill-fated ship. "I moved to the island to stay with my dad for a while."

Bailey Jo flashed her brilliant white smile. "That's right! I know your dad – a little. I'm friends with his girlfriend's daughters."

"You know Sheila?"

"Yes, they're all so nice. Mackenzie helped me find a place to stay here on the island. I'm Bailey Jo."

Mia grinned. "I know who you are, but it's nice of you to introduce yourself."

Bailey Jo sighed. "Are you sure you're okay?"

"I'm fine. Just clumsy." She paused. "I'm sorry. I heard you and was trying to give you some...uh, privacy."

"Oh." Bailey Jo let out a breath. "Yeah. I'm having a private pity party. A mountain boo-hoo, if you will."

"Don't let me stop you," Mia said, putting up her hands and laughing.

It was a nervous laugh. Even though her parents were technically famous, other famous people made her nervous. Her mom had always kept them away from that world, wanting them to stay grounded.

Mia had been glad for it at the time, though she felt like a dope now.

"Are you – is everything okay?" Mia asked.

Bailey Jo swiped a hand to her face. "I'm done crying, if that's what you mean. I got it all out."

Mia winced, slowly lowering herself onto a rock. Maybe if she loosened the laces of her hiking boot, she'd be able to walk normally. "Sorry. I didn't mean to intrude."

"You're not." Bailey Jo took a seat next to her. "I didn't mean to come up here and have a pity party. And yet, here I am, snot shooting out of my nose..."

Mia pulled a brown napkin out of her pack and handed it to Bailey Jo. "I was coming up here to do the same thing. Minus the snot, maybe."

"Really?" Bailey Jo blew her nose daintily. "I guess the mountain called to us."

Mia's bleeding wasn't dainty. She wiped the flow away from her eye once, then twice.

"Did you pass those tombstones on the way up?" Mia asked. "The Royal Marines who drowned here in, like, 1860?"

Bailey Jo nodded, her face solemn. "I still wanted to go for a swim."

A laugh burst out of Mia.

"Just kidding," Bailey Jo said.

"I was sure they died trying to hike up here. I don't know who I'm kidding," Mia said, shaking her head. "I'm not outdoorsy enough for this. These hiking boots aren't broken in at all and they're eating my heels."

Bailey Jo puffed out her cheeks with a long breath. "And here I thought I was in trouble. Your shoes are eating you."

They broke into a fit of giggles. Mia had to be hallucinating, sitting at the top of a mountain with America's Sweetheart and rolling with laughter.

When they finally stopped, wiping tears from their faces, Bailey Jo spoke again. "Maybe you can help me. Does your dad know anything about investments?"

Mia shrugged. "He might. He likes boring things."

"I don't know if you've heard about this," she said, dropping her gaze, "but I'm being investigated for insider trading."

Mia's eyes widened. "No. I didn't hear anything about that."

Bailey Jo looked up. "Oh. Are you just being nice?"

"No, really." She paused. "I'm sure it's a big story. I tend to avoid celebrity news."

"Ah, because of your parents?"

She shrugged. "That and my own personal embarrassments."

Bailey Jo laughed. "What embarrassments?"

Mia took a step and winced. "I'm not going to tell if you don't already know."

"I think you're going to need some help getting down the mountain."

"I'll be fine. Really."

Probably.

Bailey Jo looked up, narrowing her eyes. "Did you hear that?"

Voices.

More people. Great.

"I recognize that guy," Bailey Jo said. "He's a police officer. I'm sure he can help you."

Mia put up a hand. "Please, no, it's fine –"

Bailey Jo already flagged them down. "Officer Kowalski! Over here!"

A guy her dad's age appeared, a scowl on his face. Just behind him, a hunky younger man, all broad shoulders and friendly grins, followed.

Mia sighed. So much for keeping her embarrassments to herself.

Two

"Bailey Jo," Hank said, rocks tumbling downhill as he approached. "I didn't expect you to follow me all the way up here."

Jacob rolled his eyes. Leave it to his dad to accuse a pop star of stalking him. He couldn't resist a dad joke.

"Ha ha, you caught me." Bailey Jo flashed a smile.

He'd heard Bailey Jo moved to the island, but he assumed it was the typical celebrity thing: buy a multi-million-dollar estate and leave it to collect dust.

She wasn't supposed to be out and about like this, dressed like a casual hiker. He glanced at her. It was uncanny, like she'd been cut from a magazine. She was so much shorter than he'd expected.

"Harassing the Chief Deputy Sheriff is a crime," Hank said, then paused. "I think."

A pity laugh from Bailey Jo.

Jacob gritted his teeth. This was too much. How far would his dad take this lame joke? Would Jacob have to jump off the side of the mountain to escape the embarrassment?

"I'm off the clock," Hank said, "so I'm not going to look into that right now."

Off the side of the mountain it would be.

"I'm glad you're here," she said. "My friend slipped and took a tumble. Can you lend a hand?"

Jacob blinked. There was a woman behind Bailey Jo, her dark hair tied into a ponytail, her forehead glossed in blood.

How had he not noticed her until now?

Probably because he couldn't tear his eyes away from Bailey Jo – or bear to look at her at all while his dad did his song and dance.

Jacob wasn't even a fan of pop music, but she was *Bailey Jo Collins!* He'd have to explain it to his dad later. She was like the Madonna of their time.

Hank squatted down next to the woman. "What happened here? Did Bailey Jo attack you? You can tell me if she did. I can take her."

The woman laughed. "No, it wasn't her. It was a tree branch. I rolled my ankle."

"And fell down the hill," Bailey Jo added, pointing.

He let out a whistle. "From up there?"

"Yeah, but I'm fine," the woman said, struggling to her feet. "It's really fine."

Hank took a step back. "Looks like you got a nasty scratch on your head, and if your ankle is broken or sprained, you can't make it down by yourself."

"It's not broken, it's –" She took a step and winced, sucking air through her teeth.

"Broken," Bailey Jo said, making a face and shaking her head. "Definitely broken."

"It's really okay. I'm fine," the bloodied woman said.

Her ghostly skin stood out against the dried blood. Her lips were two pale pink petals.

"Let us help you," Jacob said gently. "We can get you back to town."

"That's my son, Jacob," Hank said with a nod. "I have a first aid kit in my truck. Let me take a look at you."

"Yeah, you don't need to be a hero, Mia," Bailey Jo said, turning to steady her friend with an outstretched arm. "Let these big, strong men take the glory and carry you down the mountain."

Hank laughed. "You don't have to flatter us." He paused, turning his head. "You're Russell's daughter, aren't you?"

She smiled. "Yes."

"Mia Westwood, the one and only," Bailey Jo added.

"Starlight Echo!" Jacob said, pointing at her. "That was you, wasn't it?"

Her lips tightened. "Yes."

Jacob dropped his hand. "I'm sorry; that was rude. I was excited to recognize you. I loved that movie."

"Thank you." She flashed a quick smile, then looked down at her ankle.

Hank jerked his head. "He gets his charm from me. He'll stop harassing you now and will instead offer some help."

Jacob laughed. "I'm sorry. Can I give you a hand?"

He stepped forward, and Mia shook her head.

"She's going to deny it," Bailey Jo said, "but she can't get down the mountain by herself, and I'm not going to carry her."

Mia turned to her. "You know I can hear you, right?"

"Listen." Hank took off his sunglasses. "If Patty finds out I let you stumble injured and bleeding down the mountain, she will skin me alive. I don't want that." He put his hands on his hips. "There's a less steep trail around the other side. Let us guide you down. I'll make sure you don't have a concussion, and Patty won't give *me* a concussion."

Mia sighed, a smile dancing on her lips. "All right."

She turned and started to hobble down the trail.

"Not that way," Hank said. "Jacob, help her out."

Jacob stepped next to her. "It might be easier if you hang onto my arm. Or if you want to put your arm over my shoulder, I can keep the weight off your leg."

"This is silly," she said in a low voice.

"It's not. Accidents happen. Once I was hiking here with my mom, and I gashed my head open messing around. I needed staples."

She winced. "What?!"

"I was ten." He smiled. "Bled the whole way down."

"Your poor mom."

"Yeah." He lowered himself slightly. "You don't want to put too much weight on your ankle before you can ice it. Trust me."

Mia sighed. "You're right." She slid her arm around his shoulders. "Thank you."

She smelled like flowers – and onions? In a pleasant way, like a hearty lunch.

They started down the trail behind Hank and Bailey Jo.

"By the way," Jacob said, "Who's Patty?"

Mia's eyes were down, focused on her steps. "She's a tough old grandma who regularly threatens your dad."

"Doesn't really narrow it down," Jacob said.

She laughed. "She's not my grandma. Not technically. She's my dad's girlfriend's ex-mother-in-law."

"Dad's girlfriend's ex-mother-in-law," Jacob repeated slowly.

"My honorary grandma," Mia added.

"That's a good title. I'd like an honorary grandma."

"She's always accepting new applicants," Mia said, glancing up at him.

He grinned. "I'll be sure to apply."

They worked their way down the trail, weaving through the switchbacks encased with sweeping views of golden grass blowing in the wind.

Jacob had always loved this hike. There were so many ways to go up and down the mountain. It never got old. When his mom was sick, he took a picture for her at the top, then printed it and hung it by her bed. She'd said she loved to look at it when she was stuck inside, that she could feel the wind in her hair.

Once they were back on flat ground, Mia insisted on hobbling along beside him on her own. He caught her once when she tripped over a rock, but otherwise, she got on decently.

They got to the parking lot and his dad propped her up in his truck. Jacob hung back with Bailey Jo while his dad completed the customary checks for a concussion and for a break in Mia's ankle.

"So," Jacob said, staring out at the trees. "How are you liking the island?"

"It's nice," Bailey Jo said. "People are kind. Lots of artists, too. Are you an artist?"

"Nah."

"What brings you here?"

That was a loaded question. He spit out the simplest response. "I grew up here, but I've been living in Australia for a while. I got a remote job and decided to stay a while."

She nodded slowly. "I see."

He was boring her to death. Jacob was good at that. He didn't have his dad's charm. Not even close.

Thankfully, she had enough charm for the two of them. She carried the conversation entirely, talking about the jam maker she'd met at the farmer's market.

Jacob listened, nodding dumbly, trying not to stare at her.

Finally, Mia was cleared, and he was free to go. Bailey Jo and Mia parted ways, and Jacob and his dad walked back to the truck.

"I didn't say anything," Hank said as they got inside. "But it wasn't easy."

"What wasn't easy?"

"You ran into two pretty girls, and you don't ask for either of their phone numbers?"

Jacob shook his head. "Not really on my radar, Dad. I know you're not aware of this, but Bailey Jo is one of the most famous singers in the world right now, and Mia Westwood is Hollywood royalty."

Hank shrugged. "And?"

He scoffed. "And I'm not interested in phone numbers. That's not what I'm here for."

"Suit yourself." He smiled and started the engine.

They got back to the house without another word about it, but as soon as they walked in the door, his dad blabbed the entire story to Jacob's step-mom, Margie.

"You didn't think of making friends with those girls?" Margie said, her mouth hanging open. "The Westwoods are very nice people, Jacob. I don't know Bailey Jo well, but it would be good for you to have some friends your age on the island."

"I have friends on the island."

"You have *a* friend on the island. Her twin babies don't count as friends," Hank said.

"Babies definitely count as friends," Jacob said. "They laugh at all of my jokes."

"Well, you could stand to add a few more friends," Margie said, patting his arm.

Jacob grabbed an apple off the counter and took a bite. "I'll take that into consideration."

Margie's pushiness didn't faze him. She had the persistent friendliness of a spaniel – and the determination, too. After Jacob's mom had died, he was afraid his dad would board up the windows and stop leaving the house entirely. It took a strong person to drag him outside.

It was Margie who had forced him back into the sun, and Margie who had made him laugh again.

Jacob had loved her from the moment he met her.

"I've been meaning to ask you a favor, Jacob," Margie said. "I need to go to the tea shop tomorrow, but my car has been making funny noises. Would you mind driving me?"

He shrugged. "Sure. What time?"

"Around noon." She shot a smile at Hank. He looked away.

"What are you two smiling about?" Jacob asked. "Is there really a tea shop, or is this a trap?"

"There's a tea shop," Hank said. "You'll like it."

"All right. Noon it is," Jacob said. "See you then."

Three

Hiding her embarrassing fall proved an impossible task. Mia managed to convince Chief Hank she could drive herself home, but when she opened the front door and tried to sneak inside, Sheila immediately yelled, "What happened?!"

It was Chief's fault. He'd insisted on affixing a bandage to her head, but despite his best efforts, one side of the bandage refused to stick to her dirt-covered skin. It made her look like she'd escaped from a hospital bed.

"It's nothing," Mia said. "I tripped when I was hiking. It looks worse than it is."

She couldn't blame Chief. It was her fault for pretending to be outdoorsy. It didn't matter that she'd bought the gear and looked the part. Mia's outdoorsy limit should've been taking that sub on a picnic at the dock.

Except then she might've fallen in the water...

Sheila put a delicate hand on Mia's chin and scanned the damage. "It looks frightening. And you're limping!"

Her ankle throbbed. It didn't like moving, but it didn't like not moving even more. "Just a sprain. I think."

"Can I see?" Sheila asked.

"I'm afraid to look at it. I'm imagining it's all purple and twisted and swollen..."

Sheila got down on the floor and gently pulled down Mia's hiking sock. "It doesn't look too bad. It's a normal color, but I see some swelling."

Mia peeked down. The ankle was puffy, unnaturally protruding at the sides, but not grotesque. "That's good. I'm sure it'll be fine."

"It will be." Sheila walked her to the couch. "Sit down."

Before Mia could say a word, Sheila wrapped, washed, and sterilized the cut on her head, then wrapped her ankle with a cold bandage.

"You really didn't have to do all of this," Mia said.

A mug of tea appeared in her hands, and a hint of orange drifted up to her nostrils. She took a deep breath and released her shoulders.

"Please. You made me feel useful for a minute." Sheila paused, smiling. "I've got skills, you know. Maybe next time you go hiking, you should take me with you."

Mia leaned forward and grabbed a biscuit. "I'd love to go hiking with you, but there will not be a next time."

Sheila laughed, but Mia meant what she said. Both parts. She was done trying to be outdoorsy. It was too bad, because hiking with Sheila probably would be fun.

Mia had surprised herself when she first met Sheila. Sheila was *truly* lovely. Mia actually liked her, and living on the island shocked her even more.

It had been strange when her parents divorced at first. Her mom had started dating right away, which made Mia spitefully resentful at any hint her dad might bring around another woman.

Until he didn't. Then Mia's worry grew in another direction – her dad being alone forever. He seemed all too happy to spend his time chasing wolves in Yellowstone. That was no way to live life, lying in a snowy ditch and ranting to strangers about pack dynamics.

All Mia wanted for her dad was to find someone who was kind, and Sheila had knocked it out of the park. The fact that she was an artist in her own right – a musician – and she had four daughters was a bonus. Mia had always wanted a sister, and now she could have *four?*

She knew Eliza best, since she lived on the island too, but all of them were welcoming and fun. It was a truly magnificent and unexpected turn in Mia's life.

After icing her ankle, her fears of a sprain faded. The swelling wasn't too bad, and the bruising seemed minor. Sheila kept her company on the couch, laughing herself into a snorting fit over Mia's retelling of meeting Bailey Jo and her unfortunate tumble.

When her dad got home that night, Mia was barely able to get the story out again, the two of them were laughing so hard.

"You both must've suffered some sort of head trauma," he said, staring at them. "Nothing else could explain this hysteria."

Mia rolled into Sheila, tears streaming down her face.

"I think," Sheila said slowly, "it's time to send Mia to bed."

"That's not a bad idea." Mia stumbled to her feet, falling into her dad. "Excuse me."

"What did you put in that tea?" Russell asked, shaking his head.

"Nothing," Sheila said, wide-eyed. "I slipped her some Motrin in a slice of cheese, though."

Mia snorted again. "Good night, everyone. I am out."

The next morning, Mia set out for the tea shop slowly but steadily. Her ankle felt much better, but the rest of her body awoke with protest – ribs that ached with every breath, a stiff hip, and a crick in her neck. She'd spent all this time musing on how violent launches were. Meanwhile, catastrophic falls were even more violent.

She didn't love her odds.

Gingerly, Mia walked uphill, the sky a mass of grey above her and the sea hidden under a film of fog.

Eliza was out of the shop today, flying around with her pilot boyfriend Joey. Their plan was to fly to a remote mountain for camping and hiking.

A shudder ran down Mia's spine. Eliza was far more experienced with the great outdoors, but surely she couldn't be enjoying this weather? Maybe she'd come back and spend the day with Mia after all. That would be much nicer, inside with a cup of tea and a plate of cookies.

She pushed open the door to the cozy tea shop.

"Good morning," Mia called out.

Patty emerged from the kitchen, a tray of enormous chocolate chip cookies stacked three levels high. "Hello, dear! I didn't know if you'd make it after your tumble. Margie told me all about it."

Mia pulled off her coat. "Who is Margie and how does she know I fell down?"

Patty smiled. "She's part of the island network. Get used to it. News gets around fast."

Mia laughed. "Obviously."

"Cookie?"

Mia paused. Her agent had not-so-subtly hinted she needed to lose weight, telling her she'd see more roles offered to her "once she got that slimmer figure."

"No, thank you." Mia picked up an apron and tied it behind her waist.

If she wasn't going to increase her level of physical activity, the least she could do was not eat extra cookies, no matter how badly she wanted them.

Her coat would smell like cookies after she left. That was something.

"Margie is Chief Hank's wife," Patty said, setting the cookies down. "She's a dear friend and a lovely person. She's going to stop by later to check on you."

This was getting to be too much. "Please tell her I'm fine and there's no need to –"

Patty waved a hand and disappeared into the kitchen.

Mia sighed. To think she'd moved to the island for privacy.

It wasn't a busy day, but every time the door opened, Mia jumped, fearful that this Margie would make good on her promise.

It was mortifying enough that she'd stepped out of her comfort zone and rolled directly into the trunk of a tree, embarrassing herself in front of a mega celebrity and Chief's rugged son. Did people have to keep bringing it up?

Thankfully, no one knew why she'd fled to the island in the first place. That was where the real shame was: Mia circling the same thoughts over and over, thinking about herself and her career and still being too naïve to realize she was chunky by Hollywood standards.

Her mom had insisted it was healthy to take time to focus on her career and to think about what she wanted. To Mia, though, it felt like navel-gazing. Self-indulgence. The last thing she wanted to be known as was a bratty Hollywood nepotism kid. She wanted to live a life of substance – she just wasn't sure what would make it up yet.

Maybe it wasn't *always* navel-gazing to think about oneself. Perhaps she'd used that as an excuse to avoid looking inwards at all, to avoid self-reflection. That could explain how she'd managed to get through college and still have no idea what she wanted to do with her life.

It was no use fighting a battle on two fronts, though. If she was going to have to look within and be uncomfortable, she at least deserved a treat.

She picked up one of Patty's still-warm jumbo chocolate chips and took a bite.

The door jingled and Mia looked up. "Bailey Jo!"

"Hey, Mia!" She strode toward the counter, dressed from head to toe in a white velour jumpsuit. Her white boots reached her knees and were topped with faux fur, and on her head sat a white winter cap topped with a puffy ball. "I was hoping I'd find you here."

Mia set the cookie down. She'd spent the evening promising herself that if she ever ran into Bailey Jo again, she wouldn't act like such a goober. "Please don't tell me you've come to check on my injuries. I honestly can't take any more embarrassment about that."

Bailey Jo laughed. "No, I came here for entirely selfish reasons. I wanted to talk to your dad – you know, about the investments?"

"Right. You have real problems, not just a twisted ankle." Mia pulled her phone out of her back pocket. "Let me send him a text. I think he's over at the sea pen site. I can see when he'll be back."

"Thank you! I appreciate it."

The door jingled again. This time, Mia was delayed in looking up.

"You must be Mia!" a voice called out.

She sucked in a breath. A woman in a yellow rain coat stood there, smiling broadly, her cheeks red and rosy. Behind her stood Jacob, scratching the back of his neck and looking down.

"I am," Mia said. "Let me guess..." She tapped her chin. "You're Margie."

She grinned. "Guilty! Did Patty tell you I was coming?"

"She did." Mia hit send on her message and smiled. "It's nice to meet you. And it's nice to see you again, Jacob."

His arm jutted up, then down, in a hasty wave. A pained smile crossed his face before he looked down again, studying the display case of baked goods with renewed intensity.

It had to be because of Bailey Jo. As delightful as she was, she was far too famous to feel normal around. Mia had only managed to respond somewhat normally then because she'd practiced it all night, the way she'd learned to in school debate class.

At least someone here was more uncomfortable than Mia. It took the pressure off.

"Good to see you, too," Jacob said, eyes glancing up for a moment. "How are you feeling?"

"As good as new," she lied.

He nodded. "Glad to hear it."

"You need to be careful!" Margie barked, pulling off her jacket and hanging it by the door. "If you stumble off some of these trails, you'll end up in the ocean!"

That would've been preferable to what had happened, being swept out by the sea, but Mia nodded anyway. "I think I'll take a break from hiking for a while."

Bailey Jo laughed. "Hi, Margie."

"Hey there! What brings you to the tea shop?"

"Oh, you know," Bailey Jo sighed, "looking for a place to hide my shame."

"Well, a tea shop is as good a place for shame as any other, I suppose," Margie said.

"I'm only kidding." Bailey Jo drew herself up and turned to Mia. "I decided after yesterday that I'm not going to be humiliated about this anymore. I'm not going to hide. I've done nothing wrong, and I need to face it head on."

Mia raised her eyebrows. "Bold. I like that."

"I'm not sure I follow, but I support you," Margie said with a nod.

"It's much more my style than that boo-hoo I had on the mountain." Bailey Jo rolled her eyes. "Who has time for pity parties anyway?"

Mia grinned. It was getting harder to hang onto her shyness around Bailey Jo. She was simply too charming. Probably why she was such a big star.

She went on. "My lawyer told me to sit tight, but I'm sure Martha Stewart's lawyers told her the same thing."

"Martha Stewart?" Jacob looked up, a half-smile on his lips. "Have you been insider trading?"

"I have not, but I'm being accused of it," Bailey Jo said.

The smile evaporated from his face. "Oh. I'm sorry. I was making a joke. I had no idea."

"It's fine." Bailey Jo waved a hand. "I'm going to figure this out. I need to talk to Russell and see if he's worked with Quantum Extend. I was led to believe everyone in Hollywood did."

"Quantum Extend?" Jacob asked. "What about them?"

Bailey Jo turned to him. "Do you work in investing? Maybe you can help me."

He shook his head. "I'm just cloud engineer, but I've worked with the company. They're great."

Bailey Jo frowned. "Yeah. I thought so too. Until recently."

The kitchen door swung open. Patty pointed a finger at Margie. "Hello! I've got that new tea set you wanted to see."

A smile spread across Margie's face. "New tea set! Yes! Thank you! Please excuse me, I'll be right back."

Mia tilted her head and Jacob caught her eye. They both seemed to have the same thought – this was a setup – but the moment passed when Bailey Jo spotted the cookies.

"Oh my, those look good."

Mia nodded. "They are. Can I get you one?"

"Yes, please!" She clapped her hands together.

Mia smiled to herself. She'd made the star-approved choice on the cookies after all.

Four

As soon as the door shut, the whispering began.

"They had no idea I would bring Jacob!" Margie said.

Patty beamed. "None!"

It was time to set the water to boil. Patty had planned to bring out a pot of tea, and they'd have no choice but to share it and chat with each other.

This was one of the best parts of owning a tea shop. It wasn't about the delicious teas, or the beautiful tea sets, or even the baking – which Patty loved, too. It was about bringing people together.

Forcing them together, if need be.

"I didn't know Bailey Jo would be here," Margie mused. "That was a nice bonus."

Patty nodded, scooping the loose black tea into the strainer. "Bailey Jo likes to stop in once in a while. Seems like a nice enough young woman. She and Mackenzie are friends."

"According to Jacob," Margie said, putting her hands up, "she's one of the biggest pop stars in the country. I like her music, but I had no idea."

"I can't listen to any of those new songs." Patty shook her head. "It all sounds the same to me."

The kitchen door swung open and they fell silent.

Sheila stood, her head tilted. "Hello."

"Hi, Sheila!" Margie said.

Patty nodded a hello. "Morning."

"What are you two plotting?" Sheila asked, eyes narrowed.

"Nothing!" Margie's voice was high-pitched and laden with guilt.

"Nothing to worry yourself about," Patty said, pouring the boiling water into the teapot.

Sheila sighed. "Does it involve me? Just tell me now. I won't fight it, but I'd like to know."

"No, this one is for Jacob," Margie said.

"Oh." Sheila leaned against the counter. "That's fine with me, then."

Margie went on. "He needs friends. Hank is worried about him, and I am too, frankly."

"What brought him back to the island?" Sheila asked.

"He just went through a divorce," Margie said, her voice barely above a whisper. "He dated the woman for years. They seemed happy. We visited them in Australia. They decided to get married on a whim, and three months later, she left him. Packed up her things and disappeared."

Patty let out a sigh. "Happens all the time."

"Does it?" asked Sheila. "What was the reason?"

"There's no reason that could justify acting like that!" Margie threw her hands up. "Jacob won't talk about it. He asked if he could stay with us, and of course we said yes. We love having him. He quit his job and found a new one here, which was good. But he spends all his free time helping Annie."

"Do I know Annie?" Sheila asked slowly.

"Probably not," Patty said. "There's another story." She tossed a rag over her shoulder. "I've known Annie's mom for years. They're islanders."

"Annie went to school with Jacob," Margie added. "They were in the same year and close friends."

"She's a delight, just like her mom," Patty said. "She was married a few years and was expecting twins, so she and her husband moved here to be close to Annie's mom, and to enjoy a quieter life outside of the city."

"Terrible," Margie muttered, her eyes downcast.

"What happened?" asked Sheila.

Patty sighed, pulling the tea strainer from the pot. "They bought a house, she had the twins, then two months ago, her husband decides he doesn't like island life, or father life, so he left!"

"So Annie and Jacob both got dumped?"

"Yes, but Annie isn't divorced. Not yet," Margie said. "Her husband claimed he had an important work project and they'd figure things out after a short separation."

Sheila groaned. "So he left her with the kids. Twins, too. That can't be easy."

"Of course it's not easy. What kind of a man leaves his ten-month-old babies and runs off to Seattle?" Margie pulled her phone out of her pocket and held up a picture of two fat-cheeked babies. "Look at them! They're beautiful!"

"Aw," Sheila grabbed the phone. "Their fat little arms!"

"Their fat legs are to die for, too." Margie looked at the picture and sighed. "I think that's why Jacob came back. Or at least, it's part of it. He and Annie grew up together, running these beaches and hiking the hills. She told me that one night, she called him up to tell him about her husband, and he asked how he could help. She joked, 'Are you free at four AM?' And the next week, he was here!"

Sheila raised her eyebrows. "Wow. Is he staying with her? Like a live-in nanny?"

"A male nanny?" Patty mused.

"A manny," Sheila said with a smile.

Margie shook her head. "No, nothing like that, but he helps all the time. He watches them while Annie studies, does the daycare pickups and drop offs, that sort of thing. She's getting her master's and is quite busy. I help when I can, too, though Annie hates asking for help."

"The martyr mother," Sheila said. "Been there."

"I don't know what Jacob's wife's problem was. He's clearly an angel," Patty said firmly, forcefully loading a tray with teacups.

"Yeah. Sounds like she blew it," Sheila said. "More importantly, you need to introduce me to Annie so I can babysit. I love babies."

"There you go," Patty said with a nod. "Maybe you can watch the babies so Jacob has some free time to focus on his own life and make some friends."

Sheila crossed her arms over her chest. "Friends? With Mia? Or Bailey Jo?"

Patty shrugged. "Why not both?"

A smile crossed Sheila's face. "I'm not naïve enough to think either of you are willing to stop at friendship."

Margie drummed her fingers on the table. "You know, Sheila, if you're not with us, you're against us."

Sheila laughed. "I'm neutral, but I wish you the best of luck." She picked up the tray of tea and carried it out of the kitchen.

Patty smiled to herself. "Neutral, ha. She played right into our hands, carrying the tea out for them like that."

Margie laughed. "You're a master, Patty."

"I know." Patty sighed. "I really am."

Five

It was obvious by Margie's casual greeting that she was unfazed by Bailey Jo's pile of platinum records and Mia's stunning good looks, but try as he might, Jacob couldn't shake the feeling of hyper-awareness about who he was talking to.

Not that he was adding much to the conversation.

"If they can do it to Martha Stewart, they can do it to me," Bailey Jo said. "She was the first self-made female billionaire, and they went after her for selling two hundred thousand dollars' worth of stock. All while Bernie Madoff was running the biggest Ponzi scheme in the history of the world right under their noses."

Mia made a face. "Was Martha part of Bernie Madoff's thing?"

"No, of course not!" Bailey Jo leaned forward, her hands clutching her teacup. "That was a man who stole sixty-five *billion* dollars from investors! There were literally people begging for him to be investigated, because his scam was so obvious, and nothing happened. He literally managed to steal sixty-five billion dollars before his sons turned him in!"

"Whoa." Mia looked at Jacob. "I didn't know that. Did you?"

Jacob cleared his throat. "I knew about Madoff. I didn't know the details of why they'd gone after Martha Stewart."

"Exactly!" Bailey Jo said, pointing at him. "They made it seem like Martha was some career criminal. She sold a single stock and was accused of insider trading, but they had no evidence. They couldn't convict her on it. They convicted her on lying to the police."

Jacob had been young when that whole ordeal went down. He remembered people making endless jokes about Martha in prison, but he'd never actually wondered what she'd done.

He smiled.

"What's so funny?" Bailey Jo asked.

"Nothing," he said quickly. "I never realized all the media craziness was going on at the same time as Bernie Madoff's stuff."

Bailey Jo sat back, nodding. "It's ridiculous. Instead of going after real criminals committing real crimes –"

Mia interrupted. "He stole that money from regular people?"

"*Yes!*" Bailey Jo slammed her hand on the table. "He had a lot of rich investors, but he had a lot of middle-class investors, too. They trusted him with their life savings and he made it all disappear."

"Wow. That's awful." Mia shook her head.

"I know. And you can argue about if Martha actually had any insider knowledge before she sold off that stock," Bailey Jo said, "but in the end, she hadn't harmed anyone."

Jacob drained his teacup and set it back on the saucer. It was time to make an exit. He could agree with Bailey Jo up to this point, but if she was going to confess to insider trading and argue that it was a victimless crime, he needed to get out of there immediately. He had no interest in being called as a witness in her upcoming trial.

He was about to stand when Sheila returned with a three-tiered stand of treats. "Cookies, scones, and tea sandwiches," she said, motioning to each level.

"Oh lovely! Thank you, Sheila," Bailey Jo said.

She handed him a plate, and not knowing what else to do, he sat with it in his hand.

"Enough about Martha Stewart," Mia said, a smile dancing on her lips. "What exactly is going on with you? What did they accuse you of?"

Bailey Jo took a bite of scone and let out a sigh. "I was at an afterparty for the Grammys last year and I was introduced to Ronan Devereux by a friend. He's the CEO of Quantum Extend."

There was a name Jacob hadn't heard in a while. Ronan was a wunderkind in tech. Jacob had almost gotten a job with them, but after *seven* rounds of interviews, they stopped contacting him and he saw the position had been filled.

Not his favorite interviewing experience.

Bailey Jo went on. "My friend told me I had to invest with him, that he's a genius. I met him—he seemed a bit eccentric, but nice enough. He told me he didn't think he had space to take on my account."

The features on Mia's face scrunched. "What? He was playing hard to get?"

"Yeah, it seems that way now." Bailey Jo shook her head. "I saw him at another party a few weeks later, and after talking for an hour, he said he'd take me on as a client. So, like an idiot, I wired a bunch of money to Quantum Extend and forgot about it.

"Until now, of course. My attorney was contacted for comment. He said whatever sales Quantum Extend made are being investigated for insider trading!"

"Oh, that's it?" Mia shrugged. "It wasn't you, though. It was the company. How can that be your fault?"

Jacob nodded. "Maybe they're doing their due diligence."

Bailey Jo shook her head, the fluff ball on her hat bouncing wildly. "Have neither of you been listening? I've got a target on my back!"

It was hard not to laugh at the ball on her head. The rest of it was very serious, but the fuzzy ball bouncing around...

Jacob picked up a cucumber sandwich and hid his face behind it.

"Of course I didn't do any insider trading," Bailey Jo said. "I don't do *any* trading. I didn't even know how to invest anything before this. It was embarrassing. I put it all into an account and let it rot." She paused. "Well, not all of it rotted. I also like spending it. Fashion calls to me, you know."

Mia laughed. "That's not a crime."

Bailey Jo put her face in her hands, her voice muffled. "It sounds like a joke, though, doesn't it?"

"It's not a joke," Jacob said. "I don't know exactly how Quantum Extend works. No one does. They have a proprietary algorithm that tells them how to invest. Something with AI, and from what I've heard, it can't be beat. Maybe that's what's being investigated."

Bailey Jo dropped her hands from her face. "Then why are they coming after me?"

"I'm not sure." Jacob took a sip of tea. He wanted to offer words of encouragement, but what did he know? Maybe someone did have it out for Bailey Jo, or maybe in her ignorance, she'd done something illegal.

"I think I can help," Mia said slowly. "At least in finding out some information. I have a friend who has a certain set of skills."

"Skills?" Bailey Jo leaned in. "Is this friend a spy or something?"

Mia laughed. "Not exactly. He's a digital private detective."

These cucumber sandwiches weren't half bad. Jacob swallowed another bite before asking, "What does that mean?"

"He's a hacker," Mia said, her eyes shut. "It's a fancy way to say he's a really good hacker, okay? He has access to information that other people don't."

A laugh sputtered out of Bailey Jo. "Like, legally?"

"Technically, yes, it's legal," Mia said.

Jacob narrowed his eyes. "Are you sure about that?"

"I trust him, so yes." Mia turned to Bailey Jo. "Do you want me to see if he knows anything about that company and what they do?"

Bailey Jo sat back, biting her lip. "As long as you tell him not to do anything illegal, then yes." She jutted a finger into Mia's face. "I mean it. Nothing illegal, extra-legal, or questionable. I don't want to get in any more trouble."

Mia set her teacup down, a grin on her face. "I promise. Scout's honor."

"And you, Jacob," Bailey Jo said, turning to him. "If you know anyone else who is in the same situation as me, I want to talk to them. Outside of that few parties where I met the guy, I don't really run in that crowd."

Jacob didn't run in that crowd either. In fact, he tried to avoid crowds as much as possible. "Sure thing."

Margie emerged from the kitchen, a broad smile on her face. "Oh lovely. You're all having tea."

There was his chance to get away from this disaster. Jacob stood. "I've actually got to get going, Margie. I'm supposed to babysit the twins in half an hour."

"That's right!" She clapped her hands together. "It was great seeing you all. We'll have to come back again soon."

Not Jacob. He wouldn't be coming back, hopefully ever. One more conversation with Bailey Jo and he'd be subpoenaed to testify; he could feel it.

"Take care," he said with a smile and a wave.

Six

I t wasn't a busy day at the tea shop. Mia and Bailey Jo managed to eat their way through a second tiered stand of treats and drink two more pots of tea. Occasionally a customer wandered in, and Mia helped them while Bailey Jo hid out of sight, the furry white ball on top of her head the only part of her that was visible.

It was a grand time. They got off the topic of stocks and onto everything else – favorite movies, embarrassing moments as tweens, and Bailey Jo's charity back home in Kentucky.

It was an animal shelter, first and foremost, but it also provided free services – a clinic, food, medications – to help people keep their pets at home when times got hard.

"I'll never forget when my mom had to give up our dog," Bailey Jo said, her eyes glassy. "We were flat broke, on the verge of being homeless. We had food stamps for ourselves, but nothing to feed him. She sobbed into his fur for an hour before dropping him off at the shelter."

Six years later, Bailey Jo had her first hit, and after an expansive search, she found their old dog. Miraculously, his elderly owner had to move in with his daughter and was desperately looking for a place the old boy could stay. Bailey Jo had brought him home to her mom with a big red bow on his collar.

"None of us could stop crying," Bailey Jo said with a laugh, blinking away tears. "He was slower and more grey in the muzzle, but he still jumped up to kiss us. He hadn't forgotten us at all."

It was the first time Mia truly forgot about Bailey Jo's stardom. Beneath her whip-smart career moves and the beautiful storytelling in her songs, she was only human – a hilariously unguarded, unapologetically stylish woman with a southern drawl and a beating heart for animals and kids.

She was not someone who would try to scam the system with insider trading. It was absurd to even joke about it.

Bailey Jo left after closing, and Mia immediately contacted her hacker friend. He'd been so helpful when Adelaide was in trouble, so surely he'd be happy to help Bailey Jo?

She called – he preferred not to have things in writing – and explained the situation in a message.

That night, her mind wouldn't let her sleep, instead going over the facts Bailey Jo had shared. The accusations had to be a mistake. Insider trading was cheating, and Bailey Jo didn't have a cheating bone in her body. She owned her vices – expensive clothes and vanity about her hair – but grew up far too poor to know how to pull Wall Street tricks.

Eventually, Mia slipped into a dream about a courtroom where she sat and watched as Bailey Jo strode in, head held high, wearing head-to-toe pink like Elle Woods. Dream-Mia unclenched her hands and sat back with a smile.

. . .

The next morning, she woke groggily and grabbed at her phone, dropping it, then stooping to pick it up. Her hacker friend had returned her message.

It was a short voicemail. She hit play. "Hey, I'm sorry, but I can't help you with this. In fact, I wouldn't touch it with a 1200-foot pole, and you shouldn't either."

Mia played it twice, blinking as she strained to listen, then called him back. It went to voicemail, and she debated leaving another message, but ultimately didn't. There were only so many favors she could ask.

She got ready quickly and rushed to the tea shop. She was still covering for Eliza for a few more days, and really, her focus needed to be there.

But all she could think about was that warning. Between pots of tea and chit chat, she snuck into the kitchen and looked up everything she could find about Ronan and Quantum Extend.

The company and its technology was an enigma, its website plastered with phrases like generative AI, deep learning, and hyper-personalized investment.

There was even less available about the CEO and founder Ronan Devereux. The most she could find was a long article extolling the expansion of his company from start-up to Silicon Valley giant.

The cover image was of a thin, bespectacled Ronan leaning against the hood of a Honda Civic, rust around the wheels. The caption read, "Despite being a millionaire, Ronan stays close to his roots."

How that was close to his roots, Mia wasn't sure. Both of his parents were investment bankers. He failed out of school in his twenties, and during the next years developed the proprietary technology and machine learning software that made Quantum Extend's famous investments.

Or so he claimed.

Mia wasn't charmed by the rusty car. The phrases he threw around sounded impressive, but what did they really mean? She spent the day reading articles and watching videos to better understand the world of Wall Street, then of AI.

It didn't help much. It seemed like Wall Street made things intentionally confusing, and AI didn't seem much better.

Surely, Mia was missing something and Ronan had to know what he was doing. Serious people had invested millions of dollars into the company and the technology. The stock price had climbed steadily since the company had gone public, and more interesting to Mia, Jacob seemed to respect Quantum Extend.

There was no evidence they'd mislead their investors. Absolutely everything she found about the company was positive, and there wasn't even a debate. Maybe that was why her hacker friend told her not to go near it. They were beyond reproach.

After slogging through definitions and articles about investment for the entire day, Mia left the tea shop feeling hopeful that the whole thing would blow over. She could see it being a case of the law misunderstanding a new technology or needing time to catch up. Nothing more. Bailey Jo was an easy target for someone looking to make a name for themselves, but it wouldn't pan out.

Then again, she couldn't ignore the thought that *someone* was up to no good. Maybe not Ronan, but someone at the company had stepped out of line and done something illegal. It wasn't impossible. Someone may have gotten greedy and saw Bailey Jo as an easy target...

That evening, she was trying to distract herself from her thoughts when she heard a knock at the door. Mia opened it to find Bailey Jo standing there, her eyes red.

"Just me," Bailey Jo said, walking through the door.

Mia stepped aside. How did Bailey Jo even know where she lived? "Are you okay?"

"I've been indicted," she said with a sob, collapsing onto the couch.

"Indicted for what?" Mia handed her a box of tissues.

Bailey Jo pulled out two tissues and loudly blew her nose. "For insider trading!"

"Wait. Does that mean they found you guilty?"

Bailey Jo shook her head. "No, not yet. It was a grand jury. That means they think there's enough evidence for me to go to trial. My attorney says not to worry, that it could take months and we have to comply and..." She blew her nose again. "I don't know what I'm going to do, Mia."

Mia grabbed her shoulder. "You're going to get through this. I'll help you, okay?"

"That's nice of you." She sniffed. "You mean you'll visit me in jail?"

"You're not going to jail!" Mia said.

"They sent Martha Stewart to jail."

Mia shook her head. "You've got to let Martha go. This is a different situation. A different world. I've been reading a lot about Quantum Extend."

"I should've read about Quantum Extend before I gave them all of my money," Bailey Jo said, shaking her head.

Mia scooted closer. "They're impressive. I'm not going to pretend I understand, but they're highly regarded and –"

"And," Bailey Jo cut her off, "they made it look like I was insider trading."

Mia softened her voice. "No. I think because it's so new, people don't understand how it works. It's just a new technology. They'll bring experts into court and it'll all sort itself out."

Bailey Jo sighed, her eyes staring straight ahead. "I'm not so sure about that."

"I am." Mia sat up straight. "We're going to figure this out. I promise. If someone set you up, we're going to figure it out. I'm going to help you."

<h1 style="text-align:center">Seven</h1>

J ust as he started toward the building, a car seat in each hand, a voice called out, "Hey, Jacob!"

Avoiding small talk was the hardest part of daycare drop off. Normally, Jacob was fine with small talk, but not when he had a baby on each arm scheming an escape.

Jacob shifted the weight on his arms. Annie really should have opted for lighter car seats. These were sixteen pounds apiece. Noel clocked in at eighteen pounds, and Leon at twenty. That was seventy pounds of baby and baby equipment rolling into daycare at once.

He turned to see who it was this time. His heart lodged itself in his throat.

"Hey, Mia," he said.

Was he out of shape, dehydrated, or still not used to being ambushed by stunning celebrities?

She was dressed to blend in, with large, square sunglasses and a baseball hat pulled low over her eyes. Her long ponytail bounced as she jogged closer.

"Oh my goodness!" she said, stooping down. "Who are these two sweethearts?"

"This is Noel, and this is her twin Leon," he said, nodding down at them. "They're my friend Annie's kids. I'm dropping them off at daycare."

Mia beamed, waving both hands, then puffed at her cheeks and blew a raspberry.

Noel burst into giggles. Leon stared at her, his brow furrowed, his lips in a pout.

Jacob suppressed a smile. "Don't mind him. He gets nervous around superheroes."

A laugh burst from Mia. "I'm sure that's it and not me acting like a crazy lady. Sorry, I didn't mean to hold you up. I could help you take them inside?"

Jacob shook his head. "I'm good, but thanks."

"Okay!"

He nodded a goodbye, then turned and walked into daycare. After the usual hellos, he released the twins into the chaos. Noel immediately put herself into the lap of one of the teachers, and Leon crawled toward a blanket peppered in toys.

They never gave him a hard time about leaving. To the twins, Jacob was a tolerable presence, but not a necessity. Poor Annie sometimes got stuck for half an hour, the twins clinging to her legs and wailing.

Being Mom was tough. Being Uncle J, as Annie called him, was a breeze.

He picked up the car seats and headed back to the car, scanning as he walked. His heart jumped when he saw Mia on the sidewalk.

"I'm actually glad I ran into you," Mia said. "I wanted to talk to you about Quantum Extend."

He'd forgotten about that. "Oh?"

"My hacker friend said he wouldn't touch it with a 1200-foot pole." She paused. "Which, unfortunately, only made me more interested."

He chuckled, clicking a car seat into place. "I bet."

"Can I buy you a coffee and pick your brain? I'm trying to find out everything I can about the company. I want to help Bailey Jo."

"I'm not sure how much help I can be."

She tilted her head, a half-smile on her face. "At least hear me out, then?"

"Well..." Jacob clicked the other car seat into place. He didn't have any meetings that morning, and he could stand to get some coffee.

Plus, Mia seemed relatively normal. Maybe Margie was right. It wouldn't kill him to expand his social circle. "Sure, that'd be nice."

They walked to the coffee shop side-by-side. Mia ordered first – a flat white – then moved to a table by the window over-looking the harbor. Jacob ordered a cappuccino. The barista refused his credit card.

"Mia beat you to it," she said.

He smiled. "I see."

He joined her at the table and took a seat. "Thanks for the coffee. Sneaky move on your part."

"I said I'd buy you a coffee," she said, grinning. "In exchange for information, of course."

"Of course." He took a sip. Caramel and chocolate filled his mouth. Much better than what he made himself at home. His dad insisted on keeping the world's most disgusting coffee machine. He believed that because the timer still worked and it could heat water, it was still good.

Mia set her cup down. "I'm not sure if you heard, but Bailey Jo was indicted by a grand jury."

"Huh," he shook his head. "I hadn't heard."

"She's devastated. She's convinced she's going to go to jail."

Jacob sighed. "Maybe she is. She might've done more than she's letting on."

Mia's forehead scrunched, her lips pursed. "No. No way. She didn't do anything wrong. I'm sure of it."

He shrugged. He didn't care one way or the other, but he was being realistic. "Maybe not. My dad always likes to say a good prosecutor can get a grand jury to indict a ham sandwich."

"What?" she tilted her head. "Are you calling Bailey Jo a ham sandwich?"

"No," he laughed, looking down at his cup. As down to earth as she seemed, Mia was still intimidating. A smile always dancing on her red lips. Her eyes, two clear blue pools, never leaving his face, never missing a beat.

"I'm saying," he said slowly, "it doesn't mean anything. It's a quote from an old judge. Grand juries will indict anyone. The evidence, or lack thereof, can be twisted. The defense doesn't even get to speak to a grand jury. There's only one side of the story being presented."

"Oh!" A smile spread across her face. "Look at that. You already know more than I do."

"I'm sure it stops there."

She leaned in. "Do you have any idea why my hacker friend would be so afraid of Quantum Extend, or of Ronan?"

Jacob took a sip of coffee and sat back. "I mean, it'd be like trying to hack the CEO of Apple. It's not going to be easy."

"Right. You can't just hack into anyone's phone."

"No, you can, actually." He cleared his throat. "It's honestly creepy, the type of technology that's out there now. Governments across the world can access any phone they want to – but not always without being detected. They can read your messages, get into your emails, turn on your camera and watch you sleep."

"Ew!" she whispered. "You're not serious."

He nodded. "Individuals can do it, too. It's not exactly illegal, either – it's hard for the laws to keep up."

She sat back, her stare fixed on a spot on the table. "Okay. That tracks. Very dystopian."

He smiled. "And if you start a war with someone who can hack you back..." Jacob shook his head. "You better be sure it's a war you can win."

"Yeah, that makes sense." She paused. "Is that why you think he wouldn't go near it? Not because Ronan is particularly dangerous?"

"I mean, I don't know, but every party where I've seen Ronan, he's sitting in a corner talking about computing systems." Jacob laughed. "From a hacking perspective, sure, he's dangerous, but I don't find him particularly threatening."

She raised her eyebrows. "Do you often see him at parties?"

"Here and there. I'm not much of a partygoer, but sometimes I have to go for work."

A smile spread across her face. "Are you invited to any in the near future? Ones that you could, perhaps, take me to?"

Jacob scratched the back of his neck. "Ah, I don't know."

"I'm a great date."

He sputtered a laugh into his coffee. A date with a movie star. Sure, why not? "I don't doubt that."

"I mean, it's not like that," she rushed to add. "I'm tactful."

"Tactful," he repeated. "It's not about you. It's about me. I don't want to be nosy and get myself fired."

Her eyes widened. "I wouldn't want you to get fired either." She froze, then reached into her back pocket. "Excuse me," she said, standing. "I have to take this call."

"No problem."

He watched her disappear through the front door and looked at the time on his phone. It was getting late, and he really needed to log in for work.

Then again, his boss didn't care when he worked, as long as everything was done on time, and how often did he get an invite to chat with a star?

He tucked his phone away. No need to cut a pleasant morning short. Jacob needed more practice keeping his cool around the island's new celebrities anyway.

Eight

I f it were anyone else, Mia wouldn't have stepped outside, but missing a call from her agent made her stomach sink to her feet.

"Hey, Fabio," she said brightly.

"Mia! How's my favorite starlet?"

Coffee sloshed in her gut. Catching a call from him wasn't much better. "I'm good."

Mia paused. He was the only Fabio she'd ever met in real life, and "How's my favorite Fabio?" wouldn't be disingenuous.

He was the embodiment of Hollywood: fabulous hair, veneered teeth, and clothes that cost more than her rent. He always talked fast, a subtle reminder he had little time for anything.

She wimped out. "How are you?"

"Great. Listen, I'm in the car, so I might lose you, but tell me. Did you see the interview requests I sent over?"

"Yes," she said slowly. "The first two seem good, but I'm not sure about the one where I might have to wear a bikini."

"That's an exclusive podcast," he said, his voice dipping low. "They don't let just anybody on there."

"Right, but..." she sighed. "There was something about a water balloon fight? And eating spicy soup?"

"Mia, it's a good way to show the audience how flexible and fun-loving you are. You don't know what kind of task they're going to throw at you, literally! Ha!"

Mia cleared her throat. With her luck, they'd probably throw a live fish at her. "I'll have to think about it."

"I'll book the other two for now. And listen – are you listening?"

"Yes."

"I haven't seen you posting on social media. Remember what we talked about."

She shut her eyes "I know I'm supposed to post things, but I don't know what to say."

"Look at the other successful actresses and copy what they do. Do I need to get you an intern?" He laughed. "Kidding, I'm sure you can do it. I'm gonna lose you here, so take care."

"All right, thanks," she stammered, but the line was already dead.

She pressed her hands together, her phone clutched between her icy fingers. Not the best conversation they'd had, but not the worst. Better than playing phone tag with him for days.

He wasn't wrong to scold her. She'd heard rumors of directors casting actresses who had the most online followers. It was important to someone, even if it wasn't important to her. Plus, the movie was coming out soon, and she was required to do a certain number of appearances to promote it, no matter how awkward she felt.

Her mom kept telling her the more interviews she did, the less she'd want to crawl out of her skin whenever she was in the hot seat. Maybe she'd even learn to not tell long, rambling anecdotes that had no point. Or end. Or humor.

She put her phone into her pocket and looked through the coffee shop window. Jacob sat nodding, looking up at the barista who had her hands flying.

Was the barista telling him about her problems? Was that what everyone did to Jacob? Accost them with their woes?

He had one of those faces. Placid, with a touch of polite bewilderment. He was handsome, too, in a natural way. Nothing in-your-face that looked expensive to maintain. Ruggedly handsome.

She looked away. That was enough out of her. Hollywood was making her weird. She didn't need to analyze Jacob's good looks; it was just that she was too used to seeing guys who didn't eat outside of a specialized meal plan and spent four hours a day at the gym.

Mia hated the gym. How did they spend four hours there? It seemed like torture. Maybe that was why their faces looked like that. It wasn't the plastic surgery; it was a glint of madness from hearing too many weights hit the floor.

Jacob was a nice guy. A normal guy. Who else would drive his friend's twin babies to daycare? Unless they were more than friends...

It wasn't any of her business. Jacob was being polite, but she wouldn't pressure him into helping her. He didn't need to worry about losing his job because she wanted to play investigator.

Mia pulled the door open and walked back to her table.

"I'll see you around," the barista said with a smile.

Jacob nodded. "See you."

"Sorry about that," Mia said, taking her seat.

"Are you okay?" He leaned forward. "You looked like you got some bad news."

The cup in front of him was empty. Maybe the barista had stopped by to ask if he wanted a refill. Maybe he wasn't friends with everyone, dealing with everyone's problems.

She rubbed her forehead and laughed. "It was my agent. He can't help it—he's always bad news."

"Sorry to hear that."

"It's nothing." She waved a hand. "Anyway, back to my plan. I'm going to tell you about it, and you can decide from there."

"All right."

"I want to help Bailey Jo. My idea, which admittedly isn't very developed yet, is to get a meeting with Ronan. Going to one of these parties would be perfect. I'm going to talk to him and pose as a potential investor and feel it out."

He cleared his throat. "Feel what out, exactly?"

"The technology. The company, the people. Maybe someone less than trustworthy thinks I'd be a good target, too. I'm not sure." She leaned in and lowered her voice, "But, between you and me, I'm broke."

A laugh sputtered out of him. "Sorry," he said quickly, "I didn't expect that."

"No offense taken," she said, grinning. "I don't have two pennies to rub together, let alone invest, but they don't need to know that."

Jacob sighed. "I really shouldn't have let you pay for my coffee, then."

She rolled her eyes. "You know what I mean. Well, maybe you don't, because you have a real job and you don't depend on randomly timed odd jobs to keep you afloat."

"Seems challenging, and like I should've paid for the coffee. Chivalry isn't dead, you know."

She shook her head. "No, it's just – it's fine. Don't feel bad for me. I'm a bad actress, but that's not the point either."

He laughed again. "You're not a bad actress."

"I mean," she waved her hands, her cheeks flushed pink, a laugh bursting out of her. "I'm rambling, but I'm going to bank on them assuming I've got my parents' money so they'll take me seriously."

"You don't look broke," he offered.

She smiled. That was a kind response. "Thanks. I want to get an idea of how it all works, and maybe even where Bailey Jo could've tripped up. I refuse to believe she did anything wrong."

Jacob pushed his cup aside. "Let me think about it. I'm not sure what events or parties are going on right now."

There it was. He didn't want to get near this with a 1200-foot pole, either. She couldn't blame him. It wasn't his problem.

Mia grabbed a napkin and pulled a pen from her purse. "I don't want you to do anything that endangers your job or that makes you uncomfortable. Keeping that in mind, here's my number, so you can let me know what you decide. No pressure." She slipped the napkin toward him.

"And further," she continued, "please let me know when your friend needs a babysitter. I was the star neighborhood sitter growing up, I love babies, I live nearby and have all my clearances. Even CPR!"

He stared at the napkin, a half-smile forming on his face. "That's kind of you, thanks. I'll let Annie know about your offer."

"Obviously she won't want some random woman babysitting her kids," Mia said, tucking the pen into her purse, "so bring her to the tea shop. Don't be a stranger."

He slipped the napkin into his pocket and locked eyes with her. "I won't be."

She needed to work on her pitch. And her plan. That was embarrassing, and it was time to run away.

Mia stood. "I've taken enough of your morning. It was great seeing you. Take care!"

Jacob rushed to his feet. "You too."

She pushed the door open, the air cooling her cheeks.

So she wasn't smooth. Maybe that would help her look like a target for whoever set Bailey Jo up at Quantum Extend. If someone went after Bailey Jo, how could they resist another sucker?

Yeah. Her rambling could be useful, not just a mortifying aspect of her personality.

At the very least, she might get to hang out with some babies. That would greatly improve her circumstances.

Nine

He hadn't been completely honest with Mia. There was a party coming up soon. There always was. Jacob's coworkers talked about these things constantly – the themes and outfits, the gossip and lore.

They were younger than he was. It made sense for them to enjoy all of that. He was only vaguely aware of what happened at these things, but it wasn't unusual for a big name like Ronan to show up.

Jacob spent the rest of the week debating what he should tell Mia. Her plan wasn't all that wild but, at the same time, these were people he worked with. There was no need to stir pots or poke bears. It was best to fly under the radar.

The most he could bring himself to do was tell Annie about the theme of the upcoming party.

"Gold?" she repeated.

"Gold," he said.

Annie picked up Leon and wrestled him into his car seat. "What kind of a theme is *gold?*"

"If you have to ask, you're too poor to understand," Jacob said with a smirk.

A laugh burst from Annie. "So true."

They were on their way to Jacob's place – which was technically Margie's house. His dad had moved in after he'd remarried, and he'd rented out their old house to her daughters.

It was a nice setup for everyone. When Jacob was in Australia, he'd hear about their picnics and boat trips and feel ever-so-slightly jealous. He missed island life, and it was strange to not be a part of his dad's new routines.

Now he was making up for lost time. Today was one of Margie's famous Sunday dinners, a tradition where everyone was invited for a night of hearty food and lively chitchat.

He and Annie were the only guests who could make it, but still. It would be fun, and the twins loved going over.

"At the very least, you have to go to find out what a gold theme means," Annie said, clipping Noel into her seat.

Jacob started the car. "How about you go and let me know?" he suggested.

"Ha! Yeah, right. I'd have to get a babysitter, and if I got a babysitter, I'd rather hide in my room to watch a show and fall asleep early."

He turned to look at her. "I'm available, you know. Consider your nap babysitter booked."

Annie shook her head. "Please, no. You've helped enough. Also, I'm not going to hide from my children and watch TV. It's just a fantasy."

"TV is bad for them," Jacob said solemnly. "You'd be doing them a favor."

"And it's good for me?" Annie asked.

"Yes," he said without missing a beat.

She laughed. "I guess it can't hurt me much. My brain feels like foam most of the time."

"Actually, I forgot to tell you," Jacob said. "Mia volunteered to babysit the twins, so in a weird way, this might all work out. She'll babysit, you'll fall asleep at seven with *Grey's Anatomy* in the background, and I'll go to the gold party by myself."

"Hang on." Annie slowly turned toward him. "What I'm hearing is you want to go to the party. You just don't want to go with Mia."

"I didn't say that."

"You didn't need to." She turned around, reaching to grab a stuffed giraffe Noel had dropped.

Annie could always read between the lines.

He sighed. "I don't want her to get me fired."

"You don't even like your job," Annie said. "Who cares?"

Jacob narrowed his eyes. "What does that have to do with anything?"

"You're going to run out of excuses. Horror of horrors, you might have to go to a fancy party dressed as a gold bar with a movie star as your date."

He grimaced. "Honestly, sounds awful."

"Or magical. Or at least golden."

He pulled into the long driveway. "Do me a favor. Don't mention any of this to Margie. She's convinced I need more friends."

"Maybe you do," Annie said with a shrug.

Jacob shook his head and got out of the car. His life was perfectly okay the way it was.

They got the twins out of the car and walked through the front door, the smell of onions and fresh bread and goodness pulling them in.

"Hey everyone!" Jacob called out.

The twins started shrieking, both clearly remembering what was here for them. Margie had turned her basement into a baby-proofed playroom, complete with all the excessively large toys missing from their own home – a ball pit, a jungle gym, a giant mirror running the length of the wall. She could've passed it off as a daycare.

Margie walked in, an apron bunched in her fist. "I'm sorry you came all this way, but I ruined everything."

"What's wrong?" Annie asked, rushing to her side.

"There's nothing to eat and we're all going to starve," Margie said heavily.

Hank appeared, a frown fixed on his face. "It's not that bad."

Margie's shoulders slumped. "It is. I failed all of you and I have nothing to serve for dinner."

Jacob looked at his dad. "What'd you do?"

"I opened the trash and saw the expiration date on the chicken package from two weeks ago." Hank shook his head. "I wish I'd never opened that trash."

Margie sniffed. "I had no idea. I *just* bought the chicken this morning. The store sold me old chicken! Really old chicken! I spent three hours making a beautiful chicken Irish stew. This never would've happened if I'd stuck with beef." She pinched her lips tight. "I had to throw it all away."

Jacob winced. He knew the pain of having to throw away a carefully planned, lovingly made meal. Though that was more because his ex-wife had decided she didn't like it, not because the meat was rotten.

Noel crawled to the kitchen table and nearly pulled a stack of napkins onto her head. Jacob picked her up. "I'm sorry, Margie. That's disappointing. Really disappointing, and not your fault at all."

"Why didn't I check the date?" She buried her face in her hands. "It was such a beautiful stew."

"I'm sure it was." Annie pulled her in for a hug. "I'm sorry, Margie."

"How about I fire up the grill and get some burgers going?" Hank asked. "I know it's no Irish stew, but a burger and a baked potato never steered anyone wrong."

"Unlike my chicken," Margie said with a sigh.

"Can I try to cheer you up?" Annie asked, redirecting Leon from prying open a cabinet.

"It's not your job to cheer me up," Margie said. "It was my job to feed you."

Annie laughed. "Forget about that for a minute. I've got exciting news."

"Is it that you bought me a pair of reading glasses so I can see expiration dates?" Margie asked.

"No, better. Mia is practically begging Jacob to take her on a date."

Margie gasped. "You didn't tell me anything about this!"

Jacob narrowed his eyes. Annie smiled back.

"It's not – she doesn't want to go out with me, per se," Jacob said. "She wants to talk to a guy who might be at the party."

"Oh." Margie took Noel into her arms and swayed. "So she's interested in this guy?"

"No, nothing like that," Jacob said. "She's interested in his business."

A smile crept onto Margie's face. "It sounds like an opportunity for your blossoming friendship."

Annie turned toward him, grinning. "I have to agree, Jacob. It's not every day you get to show up at a work party with a Hollywood starlet on your arm."

"She wouldn't be on my arm," Jacob said. "I don't think it's a good idea."

"Of course it's a good idea!" Margie said, clapping her hands together. "You could –"

Noel clapped once, then Leon, then they both kept clapping.

Margie threw her head back and laughed. "I'm so glad you all made it. Otherwise, it would've just been me crying tears into my poison stew."

He smiled. "Glad we could help."

"I can't wait to hear about this party with Mia, too," Margie continued.

"Oh, I don't know if I'm going to –"

Margie cut him off. "It'll give me something to look forward to. Maybe I'll try to make the stew again, even. You can come to another Sunday dinner when I recover."

There was no use arguing at this point. "Yeah, maybe."

"You can bring Mia to dinner!" Margie said. She then turned to Annie, her face bright with a smile. "Speaking of things to look forward to – have you thought any more about having the twins' birthday party here? I'd love to help."

Annie bit her lip. "I don't know. I was waiting for Roy to tell me what he wanted to do. He's being wishy-washy about the whole thing, saying we should do something on the mainland, but he hasn't planned anything."

"He's running out of time," Margie snapped. "He can plan something on the mainland and we can have something here. That's fine."

Annie sighed. "He said it's going to be hard for him to get away for work right now, and it might be too inconvenient for all the guests."

"How many guests was he planning on?" Margie scoffed.

"I'm not sure. I'm going to help Hank with the potatoes," Annie said, disappearing into the pantry.

"He has to come to the party," Jacob said, his voice low. "They're his kids! How could he miss it?"

"It doesn't seem to be his priority," Margie said. The smile disappeared from her face, replaced with tight lips and narrowed eyes.

"He's just...confused." Jacob shook his head. "Overwhelmed, maybe. Roy's not a bad guy. I've known him for years. He loves Annie. He'll figure it out soon."

"He'd better." Her voice was hardly above a whisper.

"It's not easy, but it is simple," Jacob said. "I'm not excusing what he did, running off like that. But I think he freaked out. Had a quarter-life crisis or something. He'll be back. He'll realized he messed up."

What Annie and Roy had was real, and beyond that, Roy couldn't mess up what he had with Annie. She was an amazing person, a perfect partner for him, and a doting mother.

Having twins had rocked their world. Jacob read all about how hard having twins could be, especially in the first year. It was understandable that Roy might've panicked.

Margie sighed. "I hope you're right."

"I am." Jacob paused. "Do you smell something?"

"Is it my stew?" Margie frowned. "It's poison, you know."

He laughed, sniffing Leon's diaper. "No, Margie, it's not your stew. We've got a diaper deposit."

Noel put her hands on either side of Margie's face.

She laughed, puffing out her cheeks. "Thank goodness. I couldn't take any more letdowns from that stew."

He grabbed the diaper bag. "Me too."

Ten

The days ticked by with no word from Jacob. Mia kept busy by insisting Eliza take a week-long baking class on the mainland so she could stay back and cover at the tea shop.

Every day there was a new hit piece about Bailey Jo's indictment. The media dubbed her the Millennial Martha Stewart, running with headlines like **Baby Bailey Jo Claims the Phone Made Her Do It** and **Bailey Jo Don't Know: Too Lazy to Learn Math.**

The glee disgusted Mia the most. This was an *alleged* crime, but apparently it was a foregone conclusion that Bailey Jo was not only guilty of insider trading, but also that she was a lazy, whiny baby who deserved it.

Poor Bailey Jo. She came to the tea shop to hide out.

"I can't believe they're running with this 'baby' thing," Bailey Jo said, holding up her phone. "I'm nearly forty years old!"

Mia paused. "Wait, what? I thought you were like...twenty-five."

"I'm thirty-six, thank you, and I've earned every one of my years." Bailey Jo said. "But according to them, one minute I'm barren and past my prime, and the next I'm a spoiled teenager who can't look away from her phone."

Mia's phone rang and they both jumped.

"Who is it?" Bailey Jo asked.

"I think they've found us," Mia whispered.

They burst into laughter.

"Are you going to answer it?"

Mia snatched her phone at the last second. "Hello?"

"Oh hey, hi. Mia? It's Jacob."

Mia mouthed "Jacob" to Bailey Jo. Bailey Jo gave her a thumbs up.

"Hey Jacob! How's it going?" Mia asked.

"Good. Ah, listen. I don't know if you're still interested, but there's a party on Saturday. It's in Seattle. I think Ronan will be there."

"That's great news! Does this mean...we're going?"

"It does." He cleared his throat. "There's a theme for the party. Gold. I'm not sure what it means, but I'll try to find out."

Mia didn't care. She just needed the invite. "I will bring a bag of chocolate gold coins to get in. Whatever they want, I'm there!"

"Great." He laughed. "We could take the ferry and –"

Mia cut him off. "Don't worry about the ferry. I think Joey can fly us out there, if that works for you?"

"Yeah, sure. It would save us a lot of time."

Mia couldn't stop smiling. "I'll text you my dad's address. The seaplane is tied off on the dock."

"Sounds good. See you then."

After Mia hung up, she and Bailey Jo broke into squeals.

"Look at you, infiltrating the tech world," Bailey Jo said.

"I know. I'm a pretty big deal."

Bailey Jo laughed. "Have you been to one of these before?"

"No. I've been to a few parties in LA, but I mostly hid in the corner."

Bailey Jo eyed her. "This is going to be different than an LA party."

"How so?"

Bailey Jo smiled. "I don't know—maybe I'm wrong. I'll wait to hear your take."

Mia rolled her eyes. She could care less about the party. She finally had a chance to do something. "I hope I'll have a lot to report!"

. . .

The most Jacob was able to tell her about the dress code was "fun casual with a dusting of gold." He apologized he couldn't find anything else about it, but Mia didn't mind.

She didn't need an excuse to wear a new dress – new to her, at least. Bailey Jo had insisted Mia raid her closet. She settled on a white mock neck dress, gold lace running down the sides and a golden sunrise on her back.

When else would she get to wear something like that?

Jacob knocked on the door Saturday evening and Mia promptly opened the door. He was dressed in a dark pair of jeans, a black henley T-shirt, and a pair of Nike sneakers with a gold swish.

"Subtle," Mia said, looking him up and down. "I like it."

"It wasn't my doing." He looked down at his shoes. "When Margie found out about this – through Annie, of course – the shoes showed up outside my door."

Perhaps her designer dress was too much. She looked down, eyeing the pair of platform pumps with gold sequins she'd chosen. "I hope I'm not overdressed."

"No, you look great. I wouldn't worry about it." He paused. "I fully expect the guys to try to out-do each other with how casual they are. White t-shirt, sweatpants –"

"And a watch worth a quarter of a million," Mia added.

Jacob laughed. "Exactly."

Mia looked over her shoulder. "I'd invite you in, but my dad is embarrassing and I don't want to subject you to him."

"No problem." He smiled. "Shall we?"

She wasn't kidding. Her dad had amused himself all day practicing the overprotective dad act, talking about how Jacob better bring flowers, how he needed to be prepared to answer questions about where they'd be and what time they'd be back.

She didn't know what had gotten into him. It was probably Sheila and Joey's fault for laughing and egging him on.

Mia shut the door, and a moment later, Joey and Eliza followed her outside. They were going to have a night on the town while Mia and Jacob attended the party.

Mia introduced everyone. Jacob went to shake Joey's hand and was met with a cookie.

"Sorry," Joey said sheepishly, balancing it in his mouth, "Eliza just made these."

Eliza snorted a laugh. "You didn't think to bring any to share?"

Joey chewed, eyes wide. "I'm sorry," he said, his voice muffled. "I can run and get some."

"I'm good," Jacob said, smiling.

The flight to the mainland gave them a stunning view of the islands from above. Mia and Eliza chatted as much as they could, but most of the airwaves were taken up by Joey pointing things out and cracking jokes.

She loved flying with Joey. They got the best views, and he provided in-flight entertainment.

They landed in Lake Union as the sun began to set, a stunning orange glow warming everything around them.

"We'll see you guys later tonight," Eliza said, waving.

"Don't rush," Joey added. "We've got a dinner reservation and tickets to a late comedy show."

"That's perfect," Mia said. "Have fun!"

They caught a cab to the party. It was being held in a high-rise building, the lobby shining with marble and stainless steel.

"I'd hate to fall down in here," Mia said, her voice echoing off the walls. "You could break a hip."

"How old are you that you're worried about breaking a hip?" Jacob asked.

She laughed. "You're never too young to worry about bone health."

They took the elevator to the top floor, where a girl with gold eyeshadow and gold bedazzles on her lips checked their names on a tablet.

"Exclusive," Mia whispered as they walked away.

Jacob only shook his head. "I feel like these things are just to make people feel important. That's why there's a party to begin with, right?"

"I can see you really enjoy parties," Mia said.

He sighed. "Guilty."

A guy in a white T-shirt with a thick gold chain around his neck approached them. "Jacob Kowalski? I never thought I'd see you out after dark."

Jacob took a deep breath. "Don't ruin this for me, Ryan. It's my big night out." He nodded towards Mia. "Ryan, this is Mia –"

"I know who this is." He stepped closer and slightly bowed his head. "Mia Westwood, I'm honored to have you at my gold party."

"It's nice to meet you." She offered a handshake.

He hesitated, but accepted her hand with a light grip. "Did you bring your golden ticket?"

"No, but..." Mia clicked open her purse and pulled out a gold coin. "Do you accept chocolate coins?"

He stepped back, eyes wide. "Do you have any idea how much sugar is in chocolate? Saturated fats, hydrogenated oils?"

"Uh..." She looked at Jacob.

"We'll make sure the chocolate doesn't attack you," Jacob said, pushing her hand down.

Ryan laughed. "Thanks, man."

Mia dropped the chocolate back into her purse and snapped it shut.

"If you need a snack, there's a raw oyster bar in the back. The Botox table is straight ahead—treat yourself. Do not miss the probiotic bar or the supplement dispenser. I've got my favorite brand of ayahuasca."

Mia blinked at him. "Thank you."

Ryan loudly called out the name of another guest and walked away.

Mia turned to Jacob. "How much of that was a joke?"

"None of it. Humor isn't a trait Ryan maximizes."

"What traits does he maximize, then?"

"Whatever increases shareholder value and reverses his biological age." Jacob shrugged. "We worked together a decade ago. He founded a new company and really took off, but if you can believe it, I don't know him that well anymore."

"I believe it." Mia cracked a smile. "I guess he decided I looked old enough for Botox."

"He can't imagine why we both wouldn't want Botox." Jacob grabbed champagne glasses from a passing waiter. "Excuse me, what is this?"

"A blend of fermented antioxidants and Italian grapes."

Jacob handed her a glass. "Want some expensive grape juice?"

"Sure." She took a sip. It tasted like seawater. She coughed and set the glass down. "How about we go and make some friends? I'll keep my poison coins hidden this time."

Jacob choked on a sip of the juice. "Give me one first. I need to get that taste out of my mouth."

Mia laughed, pulling a coin out of her purse. "Don't let anyone know I gave it to you."

He winked, unwrapping it. "I won't."

Eleven

There had to be at least three hundred people at this party, all weaving through the same concrete maze, tramping up and down floating steps illuminated by purple and pink and yellow lights.

It was hard not to get disoriented. Jacob focused on scanning faces. There were a few familiar ones, none who stopped to talk to him, and none he could identify who worked with Ronan.

The only people who slowed them down were the ones who stopped Mia to introduce themselves.

"I loved you as Starlight Echo!"

"Your mom is my favorite actress."

"Is your dad really living with wolves?"

Mia laughed, smiled, and posed for pictures. She was gracious, at no point giving even a whiff of annoyance, all the while pressing on to the next poorly lit room with body-shaking bass rumbling through the floor.

A picture-perfect Hollywood star. He'd almost forgotten about all of that, swept up in her charm and banter. No wonder people loved her.

After a particularly chatty fan, they got a chance to talk next to the toasted seaweed bar.

"I don't know how you do it," Jacob said. "People annoy you everywhere you go."

"They're being so nice." She paused. "It feels fake, though. No one liked me as Starlight Echo."

"Oh, come on. Obviously, they do."

"I'm not complaining," she laughed, putting her hands up. "I love compliments, even fake ones. I just know they're being kind. I've gotten a lot of feedback about how terrible I was and how I ruined the Apex Universe. And how glad people are that my character was killed off."

Jacob made a face. "You can't listen to them. It was a fun movie. I liked it."

She raised an eyebrow. "Are you a fan of superhero movies? A super-fan, perhaps?"

He shook his head. "To tell you the truth, no, but my ex-wife wanted to see it in theaters. It was nice."

"I bet she hated it."

This was the point where he should lie, but once he started talking, he didn't know how to stop. "She didn't hate it, but she had a lot of complaints. None to do with you, though."

She threw a flake of seaweed at him. "Jacob! Do you expect me to believe that?"

"It's the truth!"

His ex-wife was often unhappy with things, but there was no way to tell Mia that now without sounding like he was complaining about her.

It was just her way. He hadn't questioned it when she'd suggested seeing the movie. He just went. Bought popcorn. Held her hand. He'd wanted to make her happy.

Afterwards, she called it a waste of time. It put her in a sour mood for the entire weekend, ranting that they never did anything nice.

That was Caroline, though. He didn't know how to make her happy. He'd failed as a partner.

"Are you okay?" Mia asked. "You've got a sort of blank stare-into-the-distance look, and I'm not sure if you're having a reaction to the seaweed or what."

"Sorry." He cleared his throat. Not the time to dwell on his failings. "Are you working on any new projects?"

She scrunched her nose. "My mom convinced me to do a movie with her." Mia set down the plate of seaweed. "Completely different than a superhero movie. She's convinced it's going to launch my career."

"I hope it does," he said. "I'm no movie star, obviously, but I know what it's like to find yourself on the wrong path, career-wise."

She tilted her head. "Yeah?"

"I outgrew my position in Australia a long time ago, but I couldn't advance. To get a promotion, I needed security clearances, and to get security clearances, I needed to be a citizen."

"I see." She paused. "Was your ex-wife Australian?"

He nodded. "She got sick of me complaining about how stuck I was and agreed to marry me." He laughed. "It didn't work out, obviously."

"I'm sorry."

She didn't need to feel sorry for him. He was the one who made all the mistakes. "Don't be. I apologize for rattling on. I don't usually talk about –" He stopped. Could it be? "Hang on. I think Ronan is over there sitting on that huge pink armchair."

Mia slammed her hands down to her sides. "Really? Do I have any seaweed in my teeth?"

He glanced at her, stifling a smile. "You look great. Do you want me to introduce you?"

"You know him?" Her mouth dropped open. "You never mentioned that."

"I know him the way that anyone knows him. He's always around."

Mia ran her hands down her dress, smoothing the fabric around her curves. "Yeah. I'm ready. Wait."

"What?" Jacob turned around.

"What are you going to say?"

"I'll say you're a friend of mine and you're interested in investing with Quantum Extend."

She bit her lip. "That's a little on the nose, isn't it?"

"What would you want me to say?"

"I was hoping we could join his group and have it come up naturally."

Jacob looked at Ronan. He had an iPad on his lap. A guy stood behind him and pointed to things on the screen. "I wouldn't say conversations happen naturally with Ronan."

She grimaced. "Ah, got it. Let's go with your plan."

Jacob led the way. They reached Ronan, and he glanced up at them for a brief moment. "Hey, man."

"Hey, Ronan. I don't know if you remember me. I'm Jacob Kowalski."

He kept his eyes on the iPad. "They let you out of Australia finally?"

Surprising Ronan remembered anything about him. Maybe he was a genius after all. "Yep. Ronan, this is Mia Westwood. She's an actress, and a friend of mine. She's interested in investing with you."

Mia thrust her hand forward. "It's so nice to meet you. I've heard so many amazing things about Quantum Extend."

He offered a tepid handshake. "Thanks."

"I've been trying to read about it, but I'm still not quite getting it. How exactly does it work?" She paused. "I'm looking for a new way to invest my money."

He sighed, tapping on the iPad. The guy behind him stood silent, eyes down. "I developed a proprietary system that utilizes AI, deep learning, advanced analysis and internet scraping to decode the stock market. My customers get a guaranteed twenty percent return on their investment."

Mia put a hand to her chest. "That's incredible."

Jacob suppressed a smile. For all her talk of being a bad actress, Mia was selling it.

"Yeah, the standard barely gets to six percent," Ronan said. His eyes darted up to her, then back to the iPad. "We're not accepting new clients at this time."

Her face fell. "Oh?"

Ronan shook his head. "No."

"Well, if it ever opens up again, I'm sure my parents would be interested too. Russell Westwood and Holly Seville."

He turned around to his friend and laughed. "I bet they would be."

The friend's blank face sprung into action. A huge smile, an overly loud laugh. "Yeah!"

Mia shot Jacob a look, her forehead scrunched.

He shrugged as Ronan and his sidekick kept laughing.

Jacob delicately touched the back of Mia's arm. "Do you want to get that kombucha tea?"

"How about you get some for me?" Mia said.

"I think," Jacob said slowly, "you'll want to pick your own flavor."

She turned to look at him and he raised his eyebrow.

"Sure," she said with a sigh. "It was nice meeting you, Ronan."

He waved a hand without looking up.

They got to the kombucha table and Mia leaned in. "Why wouldn't you let me talk to him more? I could convince him."

"I didn't want you to push him too far. He's pretty touchy. All these guys are. They don't want to be questioned by any of us mere mortals."

"I thought if I fawned over him, he might tell me more."

Jacob picked up a glass of tea from a tray labeled lavender honey and took a sip. It was the first decent thing he'd found in this place. "Listen, you're very charming, but these guys aren't charmed by anyone pointing out their companies are impressive."

"He was very snooty. All 'yeah, I know I'm great.'"

"I'm not kidding about the 'mere mortals' thing. They all have God complexes. They truly believe they're better than normal humans, that they're here to shape the world. They have grand plans for how they'll change the lives of us peasants. It's disturbing." Jacob picked up a glass and offered it to her. "This is pretty good, by the way."

She accepted the tea and took a sip. "Oh, that is good." She sighed. "They can't *all* think they're gods."

He clicked his tongue. "They do. Believe me."

"I read everything I could find about Ronan, and at no point did he say anything about controlling us peasants."

Jacob took a deep breath, combing his thoughts. "I'm almost certain Ronan's in the group that believes all governments should be dissolved and, instead of voting, the richest should be in charge of us. Split the country into territories."

Mia's head snapped back. She narrowed her eyes, opened her mouth, then shut it. "What? No."

He nodded. "Yup. They have meetings about it and talk about what a utopia it would be. You can find the videos online —they're very open about it."

"Utopia for them maybe! That's, like, feudalism. What about voting? Democracy?"

"You don't need to vote. He knows better than you do." He took another sip. "Listen, they love our country, and they'd make it so much better if only all that pesky democracy got out of their way."

She put a hand to her face and rubbed her forehead. "That's too insane to process right now."

He laughed. "I'm sorry. I should've warned you. I assumed you knew. It's the new eccentric rich guy thing right now. Who knows what they'll come up with next?"

She puffed out her lips. "Why can't they pull an Andrew Carnegie and create a bunch of libraries or something?"

"I know. It's bizarre. The weirder thing is, most of the people in this room would fall over themselves to agree about how cool of an idea it is. How revolutionary."

"Guillotines are revolutionary, Jacob," she said, tilting her head to the side. "Feudalism is *so* twelfth century."

Her face was tinted by the purple lights, her smile glowing, pulling him in. His breath caught in his throat.

Jacob cast his gaze down. "Who knows? Maybe if you play hard to get, he'll come after you as a client."

"Maybe." She smiled. "Do you think there are any dance floors at this stupid party? Would the king allow it?"

He grinned. "I think we can find out."

She grabbed him by the hand. "Let's!"

He could swear he saw stars in her eyes. Jacob sucked in a breath and followed her.

Twelve

Things were moving forward with Bailey Jo's case, and it meant Mia lost her tea-drinking buddy. Still, Bailey Jo made the time to stop by the morning after the party.

"I don't care if Ronan brushed me off, or that he's crazy," Mia told her. "I won't give up that easily."

The fact that he had insane ideas about what was "best" for everyone only pushed Mia to keep going. She didn't care if people believed in his company or if they had big investors.

Something was not right with that guy.

Bailey Jo waved a hand. "Don't let him drag you into Quantum Extend. It's not worth it. I'd rather hear more about how awful this party was."

Mia laughed. "It was honestly the weirdest thing I've ever seen in real life."

She told her about the Botox table, the terrible drinks, and the anti-aging pills.

"It's not *anti*-aging," Bailey Jo corrected. "Slowing aging is a 90's idea. We're going backwards now, Mia. It's *de*-aging. It's biohacking. Get it right, or you'll turn into a grandma before my very eyes."

Patty popped her head out of the kitchen. "What's wrong with being a grandma?"

They burst into laughter. Patty grinned and disappeared back into the kitchen just as another patron walked in.

Bailey Jo ducked her head and said her goodbyes.

Mia helped the customer pick out loose leaf tea and sent her on her way. When she turned around, Patty was standing right behind her.

"Whoa! You snuck up on me!" Mia said.

"I'm too old to sneak," Patty said. "Everything I do is out in the open."

Mia smiled. "I'm still learning the tea business, so please don't hesitate to tell me what I'm doing wrong."

"You're doing everything right. Don't worry." Patty put a hand on her shoulder. "It sounds like you and Jacob got along quite well?"

"We did. He's a nice guy. Really nice."

His face popped into her mind in tones of red, orange, and blue. Lights on the dance floor, as erratic as everywhere else in that party, completely nonsensical, lighting the warm smile on his face. The music had been far too loud, but she could see the laughter on his lips...

"Can you believe," Patty said, taking a step closer, "he was married for a brief period, but his wife up and left him out of nowhere?"

"I didn't know that." Maybe the final straw had been him taking her to see Mia's movie. It was so bad it blasted their marriage apart.

"He doesn't talk about it, of course," Patty said, voice hushed. "Margie doesn't dare ask, but she worries about him. Keeping all of that to himself."

His divorce didn't seem like a closely guarded secret to Mia. In fact, it seemed like he'd wanted to talk about it.

Yet they hadn't talked about it much.

Shoot. Was that Mia's fault? Had she been rude and changed the subject when he was trying to open up? Mia sorted through her memories, the loud music ringing in her ears. She couldn't remember...

"Did you know he's helping his friend Annie take care of her twin babies?" Patty wagged a finger at her. "I bet you didn't know that either."

"I did know, actually. I ran into him with Noel and Leon the other day."

The smile dropped off Granny's face. "Oh."

Mia eyed her. "Am I missing something?"

"No." Patty threw her hands up and tossed a rag over her shoulder. "I like him. That's all."

"I like him, too."

The front door bell jingled, and a pair of customers walked up to the counter. Patty disappeared into the kitchen, and Mia seated them in the London-themed tearoom before taking their orders.

When she got back to the front desk, she finally remembered why she hadn't asked more about Jacob's ex-wife – that was the precise moment he'd spotted Ronan.

She hadn't been rude, thankfully, but if Jacob ever brought his marriage up again, Mia would be sure to listen.

It was odd, the language he'd used. He said his ex-wife "agreed" to marry him, like she hadn't been keen on the idea.

Her loss. His smile was unbelievably cute, and he had great dance moves, with neither self-consciousness nor hubris. Everyone else at the party seemed to be posturing, trying to look like they cared the least while garnering the most attention.

It wasn't like she was a stranger to posturing. Hollywood had its own brand of narcissism and insecurity, but the tech world was something to behold. The entire party felt like one long prank, a joke she wasn't in on.

Except for Jacob. He'd stood tall, like he'd been plucked off the side of a mountain, bringing the cool air and calm with him, the easy jokes, the complete lack of pretense.

His ex-wife had messed up. Big time. Her loss – and maybe Annie's gain?

Watching him wrangle those car seats had stirred something inside of Mia. There was a storyline Hollywood wouldn't touch – hunky, devoted man.

Instead, they pushed superheroes and spies jumping out of exploding helicopters. That was what men saw as heroic. They'd blow up a building for love, but not use their own two eyes to see the laundry was piling up and start a load.

What about the guy who cheerfully did daycare drop off? Who kissed feverish foreheads and wiped snotty noses? The one who took his wife by the hands and said, "You look tired, honey. Let me finish the dishes."

That's how her own dad was. Mia was shocked when she went out into the world. Her first boyfriend had expected her to come over once a week to clean *his* apartment! Like she was his maid. Or, more accurately, his mother.

Hollywood still didn't know what women wanted. Or, more likely, they didn't care. Chores don't seem romantic, but that's what life is. The drudgery of every day is life together. Mia's last boyfriend had enchanted her at first, but after six months, he looked her in the eyes and told her he didn't know how to clean the stove. "But you're so good at it, babe," he said without a hint of irony.

That relationship didn't last another week.

Mia could be projecting, but Jacob seemed like the dream guy. In her mind, she could see it clearly, the film rolling before her eyes. Annie and Jacob, high school sweethearts. He had his heart shattered; so did she. They find each other again with a burning island sunset in the distance.

"Maybe I should be a director," Mia muttered, smiling to herself.

Who would her villain be? Someone like Ronan, a guy who thought he was God's gift to earth. Meanwhile, he had nothing on the real swoon-worthy hero, a man on San Juan Island who knew how to install car seats. Even Patty couldn't help but blush over Jacob!

She smiled to herself. Mia wasn't intimidated by Ronan. She wasn't going to sit it out while her friend got bulldozed by his all-knowing technology.

As soon as she closed the tea shop, she went online to look for Ronan's contact information. It was annoyingly easy to find his email address – NumberOne@QuantumExtend.com.

If Ronan saw himself as a superhuman figure, she'd treat him the way he expected to be treated. She typed furiously, kicking her fawning up to a hundred and throwing in phrases like "once in a lifetime genius" and "marvel of our time."

It was so ridiculous she was tempted to share it with Jacob, but decided against it. He might not appreciate how pushy her closer was. "It was an honor meeting you, and I will be waiting for your response."

Two hours later, her phone dinged. Mia looked at the screen and her heart leapt. A new email!

Subject: Investment.

Mia cocked her head. It wasn't from Ronan, as she'd hoped. The sender was someone called Anonymous1200.

Hi Mia,

I hope you don't find this email too strange. I saw you talking to Ronan this weekend and I overheard him telling you about the twenty percent guaranteed returns.

This is a lie. Ronan is not able to provide that, and you shouldn't believe what he says. I think you seem like a really nice person and a great actress. You should find someone else to invest with.

- A

Mia read the email over and over, her hands running cold as she typed a response.

Dear Anonymous,

Thank you for your email. You have no idea how much I appreciate it. Is there any way we could talk more?

Mia hit send, her heart bouncing against the walls of her chest. She was onto something, and she wasn't going to stop until she got to the bottom of it.

<h1 style="text-align:center">Thirteen</h1>

Sunday was a marathon. Annie was up with Noel for half the night, the poor thing still fighting a lingering cough, and as soon as she got her back to sleep at 4:30, Leon woke up. He'd always needed less sleep than his sister and, coincidentally, one of his hobbies was getting up before the sun.

Annie managed to get them both fed and down for their first nap early, but their second nap went haywire. Noel spit up half her bottle after a bad coughing spell, and Leon promptly crawled into the puddle as Annie frantically tried to clean it up.

She needed more hands, but the best she had was a crib. Annie popped Noel into her crib, still wailing, as she quickly tried to hose the sour milk off Leon in the sink.

She was almost done with her frantic washing when Noel's cries suddenly fell silent. Annie's heart flew into her throat, sure something must have happened to her, and she swept up Leon in a towel and sprinted back to the nursery.

Jacob was there with Noel in his arms, wiping the tears from her cheeks with the tips of his fingers. "Are you jealous because you want to take a sink bath, too?"

Noel stared at him, her rounded cheeks fully rolling into a pout, and blinked.

He blew a raspberry with his lips, and she smiled. He blew another, and she broke into a toothy grin.

"Jacob," Annie sighed. "You're an angel."

He smiled over his shoulder. "I brought lunch. I texted you, but when you didn't answer, I assumed your hair was on fire."

"My hair, my house, my life." Annie set Leon on the changing pad. He rolled away, and she tickled his sides. He squealed, forgetting his plan to escape. "I slept two hours last night. And not in succession."

"How about I get all three of you down for a nap, then?"

She smiled at him and sighed. "That sounds amazing."

Once the twins were out, Annie and Jacob sat on the couch with bowls in their laps – lo mein for Annie, fried rice for Jacob – the monitor posted nearby.

"That was rough," Jacob said.

"Indeed." She shut her eyes. "Thanks for coming over. You didn't have to, but you probably cut that battle down by forty-five minutes."

"Happy to help." Jacob smiled. "One day at a time."

"One day at a time," Annie repeated. She sat back and took a breath, forcing her eyes to reopen. "How was the party?"

He kept his eyes focused on his rice, a smile spreading across his face. "Good."

Annie crossed her arms over her chest. "Interesting, considering you hate those parties and everyone who goes to them."

"Not everyone," he said.

He told her about Ryan, who had thrown the party, and the hanger-ons, and Ronan being rude to Mia.

"She didn't let it ruin her night, though," Jacob said. "She found a dance floor and we made up for lost time."

"Did you get to bust out any of the famous Kowalski moves?"

"Sure did." He grinned. "My legs hurt today. I'm too old for that."

Annie laughed. "That's so fun. I'm glad you went."

"Mia's fun." He shrugged. "Otherwise, it would've been a bust."

"But she couldn't get what she wanted from Ronan?" Annie made a face.

"Yes, her being extremely charming, gracious, and beautiful had no effect on Ronan. Or maybe because she is all these things, it made him feel powerful to be rude to her."

"That tracks." A smile crept across Annie's face. "It sounds like it had an effect on you, though. You like her."

He scraped the bottom of his bowl for two errant grains of rice. "Of course. What's not to like?"

"I haven't seen you smile this much since..." She trailed off. "I don't know. Not since you've been back to the island."

"That's not true. Leon shared his applesauce with me on Friday and that was pretty great."

Annie nodded. "Good point. You know how much he loves applesauce."

"I do."

She cleared her throat and turned her body to face toward him. "I like this for you. Forget about Caroline. Ask Mia out."

"This has nothing to do with Caroline," Jacob said. "Our divorce is final. That's done."

Final, eh? The first final decision Caroline had made in her life, apparently. "Why not ask Mia out then?"

"Come on, Annie. She's a movie star. I'm not deluded enough to think she'd want to go out with me."

"You don't know that. You're a highly eligible bachelor –"

He snorted. "Highly eligible? You sure about that? I had to propose to Caroline three times. I don't think I'm a top-tier candidate."

"That was Caroline's problem, not yours," Annie said sharply. "You should ask her out. What do you have to lose?"

He held up a finger. "My dignity." Another finger. "My sanity, chasing after someone else who doesn't really want me..."

Annie brushed his hand aside. "Don't be like that. I'd hate for you to miss out on something amazing because you're afraid."

"I'm not afraid. I'm..." He trailed off.

Annie finished the sentence for him. "Holding yourself back."

He sighed. "No."

"How long are you going to keep doing that?"

Jacob collected her empty bowl and stacked it on his. "Some racehorses are winners and some are proven losers."

"What?" She laughed. "What are you talking about?"

"Proven loser," he said, sweeping a hand over himself.

"If you're a proven loser, then so am I."

He stopped his walk to the kitchen and spun around. "You're not a loser."

"My husband left me, too."

"He's coming back. He's just busy with work, and confused, and overwhelmed."

Oh, Jacob. He was so sure of what he was saying. He thought all Annie needed was to be sure of it, too, and it would come true.

If only it were that simple.

Then again, she'd never in all her life have expected Roy to pull away – no, run away – as he had. There was a real panic in his eyes the night he told her he had to go.

"Go where?" she'd asked.

They'd just put the twins to sleep for the third time that night. All of them were sick and there was no end in sight – it had started with a cold, then maybe the flu, then pneumonia.

It was two months of nonstop, back-to-back daycare illnesses. The pattern repeated over and over. First the twins would come down with something, waking at night, unable to sleep or eat or breathe. Their fevers spiked for days on end.

Then, as soon as they were feeling better, Annie and Roy fell like dominoes, completing the cycle, the tail-end of their recovery hit with a new fever, a new stomach bug, a terrifying trip to the emergency room for Leon's breathing being off.

"I have to focus on work," Roy kept repeating that night, his voice hoarse and rattled with mucus.

It was hard for her to hear exactly what he was saying, ears plugged and head throbbing.

"It's going to get better," Annie said.

She didn't know if it was true or if she even believed it herself, but she'd had to say something. His panic had forced her to be calm.

"I haven't even been able to go for a walk in weeks," he said, mostly to himself. "We've been so sick. It never ends."

Two laundry baskets had stood stacked behind him. One was clean, one was dirty, but both were unfolded and so dug through that it was hard to tell which was which.

Every nook of the kitchen was covered – unwashed bottles, stacks of dishes, piles of mail they hadn't opened. Mountains of tissues toppled to the floor and fell under the couch, collecting dust bunnies.

"I know," she said, her voice hoarse.

"I've missed so much work, being sick and taking care of the kids, that I think they're going to fire me." Roy ran a hand through his hair, strands standing in every direction, the whites of his eyes small and red. "I need to focus on work. Make sure I don't get fired. A month or something, I think I need that. I need that, Annie. I'm at the end of my rope. I'm hitting a wall, I'm –"

He broke down into sobs then, and she leapt to hug him. "Of course," she'd said. "Whatever you need, honey. Whatever you need."

That was more than two months ago. They so desperately needed a reset, and it finally came. The fevers broke, the illnesses disappeared like the darkness in a long-awaited sunrise.

After regaining her strength after a brutal week with norovirus, it only took Annie a single day to re-tidy the house and put things in order. Peace in the house became peace within, and what was out of reach and impossible became possible. The fog lifted.

But Roy wasn't there to see it. He was still broken, unreachable. Annie was so tired she hardly had time to think straight, let alone figure out how to reach him.

Jacob put the bowls in the dishwasher and returned to the couch. "How about you go and take a nap? You look exhausted and you're talking nonsense."

She laughed. "It's not nonsense."

"Just babbling away, imagining me going from a failed marriage to dating America's Kiera Knightly," he said, shaking his head. "Go ahead. Take a nap."

Her eyelids were heavy after that meal. "Okay," she said, shuffling toward her bedroom, "but this conversation isn't done."

"Uh huh," he said. "Go."

Annie floated into her room and shut the door, her eyes already closed before she landed on the bed.

Fourteen

That week, Jacob made the trip to Seattle for an in-office meeting. It went well, and afterwards, he was sitting at his desk when he sensed someone hovering over his shoulder.

"Jacob!" a voice boomed.

He jumped. It was his boss.

Jacob cleared his throat. "Hey, how's it going?"

"I've been meaning to talk to you."

Uh oh. Here it was. He'd disturbed Lord Ronan and would now pay the price. "I'm all ears."

"Are you a fan of classical music?"

"Sure. Of course."

His boss smiled. "Great! I was thinking about the contributions you've made since you started here, and I want you to know how much I appreciate your work. You've been doing great, and I wanted to get you something as a thanks."

Coolness flashed over Jacob's chest and back. "You don't have to get me anything. That paycheck showing up in my bank account is enough."

He laughed, drumming Jacob on the shoulder. "Yeah, yeah." He pulled an envelope out of his back pocket. "I've got tickets to the Seattle Symphony this weekend. Are you interested?"

His mom had loved the symphony. They used to go as a family, Dad cracking jokes, Mom trying to educate Jacob and his sister on the composers.

Jacob reached forward and accepted it. "I haven't been in years. That'd be awesome."

"It *is* awesome. My wife and I have season tickets. Balcony seats!"

"Is that like a box seat?" Jacob asked. "Do they bring the hot dogs and Coke right to you?"

His boss nodded. "Yeah, exactly like that. Take someone you want to impress."

There was no need to go that far, but Annie loved music and deserved a night out.

He sent her a message with a picture of the tickets. "My boss gave these to me. Are you in?"

She wrote back half an hour later. "You should take Mia."

There she went again. She was like a dog with a bone. This was going to be her new hobby, joking about Mia.

"Ha, ha," he wrote back. "I think it'll be nice. Balcony seats."

This time she responded instantly. "It's kind of you to think of me, but honestly, I'd rather go to bed early. Or have a nap."

"You can't sleep your life away," Jacob wrote back.

Annie sent back one word. "Nap."

"You can nap on the ferry ride back."

Her response came almost instantly. "How about this? If Mia says no, I'll go with you."

Jacob rolled his eyes. "Fine."

He'd never do it if he were actually interested in Mia, but since he was just checking a box, he sent her a text. That way, it was easy for her to turn him down, and he could take a screenshot to show Annie he wasn't lying.

"I got these for free from my boss," he said. "Any interest in going?"

Mia wrote back ten minutes later. "I'd love to! I'll borrow a dress from Bailey Jo. And I've got an update for you about you-know-what."

Jacob blinked at his screen.

Well, that had backfired spectacularly. He rubbed his eyes and put the phone away. He needed to get back to work.

At the end of the day, he pulled his phone out again to find a new message from Annie. "She said yes, didn't she?"

He sent an upside-down smiley face and wrote back. "Enjoy your nap."

• • •

His ferry trip home was delayed, first because of an unruly passenger, then because someone parked on board couldn't find their keys.

It didn't bother Jacob. He only felt bad he wouldn't be able to help Annie with bedtime, but luckily her mom was stopping by that night.

He'd missed these ferries when he lived in Australia. There was nothing quite like them anywhere in the world. They smelled exactly as they had when he was a kid, a mix of lemon cleaner and hot chocolate and still air. He preferred them to the flashier ferries he'd ridden elsewhere.

The delays gave him time to think through the conundrum Annie had gotten him into. Was he supposed to treat this symphony night as a date? Should he make a dinner reservation? If only the symphony really did sell hot dogs in the fancy seats. That would make things so much easier.

The fact that Mia wanted to talk more about Quantum Extend made it feel very much not like a date and more like a continuation of their shared project.

Actually, it wasn't a date, because Jacob wasn't dating. He'd meant what he'd said to Annie. Some people weren't relationship material.

He and Caroline had tried to make it work for years. She even relented and married him, which was what he'd always wanted, but it had only made things worse.

Some people weren't worth marrying. Like him.

Annie tried to tie it to her situation, but that was different. Roy would come around. Those two were made for each other. When Jacob first met the guy, it was like meeting the male version of Annie. They walked in step, they never argued. They were *always* happy.

The statistics about parents of multiples were brutal, all citing the first year being the hardest. Roy would return with a fresh perspective and realize that Annie and the twins were worth the struggle, as challenging as it was.

By the time he got back to the island, Jacob's debate had been ended for him. Mia sent a message that she'd found a high-end Korean fusion restaurant and wanted to make a reservation. "Thoughts? I'd like to treat you to dinner since I'll be making you listen to my theories."

He smiled to himself. She saw him as a friend. That was good. Margie was right; having another friend wasn't a bad thing.

On Saturday, Jacob showed up at Mia's place. Again, she didn't let him to walk through the front door.

"I didn't know I was *that* embarrassing," Jacob said, shaking his head.

Mia raised her eyebrows and threw the door open behind her. "You're more than welcome to talk to my dad for half an hour about pack dynamics in Yellowstone National Park and then be quizzed about what you learned."

Jacob glanced at his nonexistent watch and sucked in a breath. "I'd hate to be late for dinner."

"That's what I thought." Mia laughed and slammed the door behind her.

Joey met them at the plane and kept them laughing during the entire flight to Seattle. There had been several mishaps at the sea pen site, the most recent being Russell falling into the ocean when getting out of the plane.

"He walked right out of his seat, phone to his ear," Joey said. "And plop! In he went."

Tears streamed down Mia's face, her body rocked with laughter. "He didn't tell me about this. I'm surprised Sheila didn't either."

"Sheila wasn't there!" Joey laughed. "I wish I had a video."

"How's Lottie doing?"

"Great," Joey said. "We think her mom will be coming back into the area soon. Fingers crossed they hear each other."

Jacob leaned forward. "Hear each other?"

"Lottie is an orca," Mia said, looking back at him. "You know, my dad's other obsession."

"Ah, that's right," Jacob shook his head, his headset rattling on his ears. "I knew about the orca being rehabilitated on Stuart. I didn't know you were on a first-name basis with her."

"You should be, too," Mia said with a nod. "You should be friendlier to your neighbors."

Jacob grinned. "Sure."

His mom would've been all over this. She'd loved the local orca pods and had always taken him and his sister out in the boat to wait for their raucous passes.

Muscles around his ribs tightened. He put a hand in the center of his chest and forced a deep breath.

It was easier to not miss his mom when he lived far away. Easier to imagine she was still here, living her life in his memories. Maybe on some level he'd known that, and that was why he'd stayed away so long.

They landed and caught a cab to dinner. The restaurant had an open kitchen and soft amber lighting. They sat at a minimalist wooden table under the warm glow, far enough from the other patrons that it felt like a hideaway.

Which was good, since as soon as they sat down, Mia told him about the anonymous source who had contacted her and warned her not to invest with Quantum Extend.

"Was that all he said?" Jacob asked.

"In the first email he only said the twenty percent returns were impossible."

"Ah."

The waitress stopped at their table. Jacob hadn't looked at the menu. Mia ordered the beef tartare and chorizo rice cakes to start.

When the waitress left, he asked, "Can you recommend something for me to order when she gets back?"

Her eyes widened. "I'd love to! If you like steak, the short rib steak is apparently to die for."

"Sounds perfect." He set the menu down. He didn't have much of an appetite. "Did your anonymous source say anything else?"

She nodded. "I wrote back and asked if we could talk. He wasn't willing to put anything else in writing, but he called me."

Jacob made a face. "Did he use a voice disguiser and sound really breathy?"

"No," she laughed, "he sounded normal, but he didn't want any of this being traced back to him."

"So much secrecy."

"Exciting, right?"

Not the word Jacob would have used.

She went on. "He said he works in the industry and he's one hundred percent certain Ronan is running a giant Ponzi scheme."

"A Ponzi scheme?" Jacob took a sip of water. "Can Mr. Anonymous prove it?"

"Well, no, which is why he told me to steer clear, but I'm thinking I should talk to the SEC and see if they'll investigate."

Jacob took a sip of water. "I don't think the SEC is going to get much out of Ronan Devereux."

"Why not? That's their job. They're supposed to protect investors."

"Ronan is a billionaire. What are a bunch of civil servants wearing JC Penny suits going to do? Ask him to comply nicely?"

Mia rolled her eyes. "He's not all-powerful, even if he's convinced you and everyone else that he is."

"How does this help Bailey Jo?"

"If he's a criminal and a fraud, it'll be easier to prove that she didn't make any of those 'questionable' trades. He did them, or he set her up! Maybe he's trying to draw attention away from himself."

Jacob wasn't sold. "But why?"

"Because his Ponzi scheme is about to collapse. That's my theory, at least." She leaned in and lowered her voice. "That's how Ponzis work. You need a constant stream of new investors to pay off the old investors. Once you start running out of new people and new money, it all falls down."

Jacob smiled. "Then why did he turn you down if he needs investors?"

She let out a huff and sat back. "I'm not sure, but Bailey Jo said the allegations against her came shortly after she told Ronan she needed to withdraw a few million dollars."

The appetizers arrived. The beef was topped with slices of pears and bunches of nuts. The rice cake was golden and glistening with bright red tteokbokki sauce and green onion sprinkled on top.

His stomach growled. Maybe he was a little hungry.

"Was she able to withdraw it?" Jacob asked, putting an appetizer plate in front of Mia, then himself.

Mia shook her head. "She was supposed to give sixty days' notice, and she did. After three months, she asked what the holdup was, and she was told her request was denied. A week later, she found out about the allegations."

"And she still hasn't gotten her money?" Jacob asked.

"Nope." Mia sat back, arms crossed over her chest. "Now you're interested, aren't you?"

"Sure, but..." he sighed. "It's still going to be hard to go up against Ronan."

Mia nodded, doling out spoonfuls of food onto the plates. "It was the same thing with Bernie Madoff. He was rich, powerful, and well-respected. Everyone who worked at his company loved him. Said he treated them like family."

"Sounds like the mob."

She snapped her fingers. "Exactly, a tight-knit family – until it all comes crashing down!"

"Did the SEC investigate him?" Jacob asked.

"I'm glad you asked, because yes. Sort of. There was a guy who kept insisting Madoff's returns were fake and he was running a Ponzi scheme. He begged the SEC to look into it, and they finally did, but they were so deferential to Madoff that the entire extent of their investigation was taking his word for it."

"For what?" Jacob took a bite of rice cake, savoring the spice.

"Basically, Madoff collected all this money and said he was investing it. Except he never did. He put it in a bank account, and when someone wanted to withdraw, he gave them money from the account."

"At twenty percent returns?"

Mia nodded. "He never even made trades! But every month, they sent investors a document listing fake trades with fake returns. If the SEC had bothered to look, they would've seen it. It was a huge, literal Ponzi scheme going back decades."

Jacob set his fork down. "So how are you going to get them to look?"

"I'm not sure yet. Maybe you can help me."

He sat back, suppressing a smile. Ponzi schemes weren't his thing. If it weren't for Mia, he would have no interest in this whatsoever.

But she was far more interesting than Ronan, and who knew? Maybe she was onto something. "I'm all ears. What's next?"

Fifteen

This was where Mia's plan faltered.

"I'm not exactly sure," she said. "You're computer-savvy, though. You know all about data storage and the cloud."

Jacob smirked. "The cloud. You make yourself sound a hundred years old when you say that."

"I'm not going to pretend I know what I don't know," she said through laughter. "Can't you somehow see what Quantum Extend is doing?"

"It's not public knowledge, if that's what you mean," Jacob said. "And having knowledge about 'the clouds' doesn't change that."

She narrowed her eyes. "I didn't say 'the clouds'! Now you're exaggerating."

He laughed. "I'm sorry. It's like in a movie when they log onto any computer and hack anywhere in the world. It doesn't work like that."

She sighed. "Can you at least look up if he's making trades? Like, what can he possibly be doing to get these wildly high returns?"

He shook his head. "If it were that easy, everyone would copy what he does. They'd all get the same returns on their investments."

"Ah. Right." Mia puffed out a breath. "I do sound dumb, don't I?"

"Not at all," he said. "The world of finance and investment isn't rocket science. It's all made up, but it's made up by them. The ones doing the trading. They make up the swaps and the rules and derivatives. It's all on purpose. Overcomplicate it so people can't see what they're doing."

"I was afraid you would say that." Mia took a bite of rice cake, chewy and perfect, a tangy sweetness and garlic melting on her tongue. "So we're not supposed to know what they're doing."

"No, afraid not." Jacob popped a rice cake into his mouth. "These are so good."

"Aren't they?"

He wasn't the sort of person to find fault wherever he went. Some of the Hollywood types she was acquainted with could be like that. Always complaining, as if it showed how cultured, how above it all they were.

"I'd only have access to those systems," he continued, "if I were an employee. I'm not a skilled hacker. Even then, if it's really fraud, it's not somewhere they would grant access to a random mid-level cloud engineer."

"Ah." Mia nodded. No one wanted to rock the boat. A tale as old as time. "Maybe you can come to the SEC with me, then.

They'll take me more seriously if I'm not ranting about the clouds."

Jacob scratched the back of his neck. "It's a small world, Mia. There's a good chance it could get back to Ronan, and –"

"And what? You're afraid he'll sue you for defamation?" Mia chanced a smile.

"More like he'll get me blacklisted from every major cloud servicing company."

She set her fork down. "That doesn't seem like the actions of an honest man, does it?"

"He's a competitive, vicious businessman – just like the rest of them. It doesn't mean he's guilty of anything. It only means he's a bad person."

Mia laughed. "Fair enough. I'll leave you out of it, but I'm still going to talk to them. I have nothing to lose."

He raised his glass. "I wish you luck. Truly."

"Thank you."

Their entrées arrived, the plates alive with color. The smell of pepper and spices filled her nostrils.

"I hope you approve of the meal I picked for you," Mia said.

Jacob's mouth was full when he responded. "The meat is so soft and the sauce is – I don't even know how to describe it. What is this magic?"

She grinned. "I'm glad you're easy to please." She cleared her throat. "So, is babysitting your only hobby, or are you really into the symphony, too?"

"Not really into it, no. We used to go when we were kids. My mom tried to keep us cultured." A smile flashed across his face and he paused his eating. "She would love what your dad is doing with Lottie, by the way. I think it's great."

"Thanks. He's doing it for all the right reasons, I think."

"Have you ever seen the orcas that live around the islands?" he asked.

She shook her head.

His face lit up and he leaned forward. "You have to see them. My mom used to take us out on the boat and we'd sit for hours—reading, playing music, having a picnic. Until the orcas swung by, jumping, splashing, calling out." He sucked in a breath. "It's the most amazing thing you've ever seen"

"I'm sure," Mia said. "I've only ever seen Lottie, and she blows me away on her own."

"She passed away a few years ago." He cleared his throat. "My mom."

"I'm sorry. She sounds like a wonderful person."

"She was." He paused. "I wasn't living on the island when they found the cancer. It spread so quickly."

His eyes were focused on a spot over her shoulder. Mia's eyes were locked on his.

"Kidney cancer," he said. "We didn't even know it was there. She didn't want me and my sister to worry about her, though. She insisted she was fine. I didn't realize how quickly it would..." He let out a sigh. "Sorry, I'm rambling."

"No, please." Mia leaned forward. "I'd love to hear more about her."

He glanced at her and flashed a smile. "I regret I wasn't here more. I should've quit my job and been here for her last months, but I wasn't."

"I'm sure you didn't know they were her last months."

"No. I didn't." He took a sip of water. "Annie was living on the island at the time. She was at our house every day, taking Mom grocery shopping, to get her hair done, or to the library. When Mom wasn't strong enough to go out, Annie cooked for both of my parents. It made me feel slightly better I wasn't here."

"Wow." Mia sat back. "Annie is...that's incredible."

"Yeah." He locked eyes with her. "Babysitting isn't normally one of my hobbies, but I'm glad I can help for once, instead of wishing I'd done more after the fact."

Mia could jump off a bridge. Who was she to tease him about babysitting? Not only was he an angel, Annie was one, too.

They were the perfect pair, and he was so gracious.

Mia chanced a smile. "I'll tell you what. Even if you won't use the World Wide Hacking System to see what Quantum Extend is doing, I'll still take you out to see Lottie. Seeing as you're an enthusiast."

A laugh burst out of him. "Deal."

They got so caught up in their conversation that they nearly missed the start of the symphony. Mia got the check and paid it before Jacob could protest, then they caught a cab and sprinted to the front doors, Mia laughing manically in her too-tall heels.

An usher escorted them to their seats overlooking the stage.

"You weren't kidding," Mia whispered. "This is fancy."

"I should've worn a tuxedo."

"Do you have a tuxedo?"

He glanced over at her. "Wouldn't you like to know?"

She laughed, covering her face. Mia fanned open the program, at first pretending to read about tonight's show, then actually being pulled in.

They were there to listen to Tchaikovsky's fifth symphony. The composer had apparently doubted himself when he wrote it, scribbling doubts like, "murmurs, doubts, laments, reproaches against..." and "shall I cast myself into the embrace of *faith???*" After the first performances, he had written a letter to a friend, saying how certain he was that it was "not a successful work," and even called it terrible.

Then, a year after composing it, he'd changed his tune, saying he started to love the symphony again, that he'd been too harsh.

In the dim light, Mia read the words over and over again. Even a genius composer could be filled with doubt; even he could look at his work with disgust and shame.

The musicians tuned their instruments, a cacophony of chaos and trills.

"They're terrible," Jacob joked. "Doesn't sound like music at all."

Mia swatted at him with her program. He laughed.

The conductor arrived to raucous applause, and the hall fell silent. She raised her arms and the music began, with every discordant instrument and musician now joining together in a perfect, dancing melody.

Her heart floated, lifting her with its questions and answers, the highs and lows, the beauty of the swelling of the notes.

For a brief moment, her mind wasn't wrapped up in worrying about herself, her movies and her career, the self-centered thoughts that made Mia so sick of herself she wanted to crawl out of her skin and start over. She focused on listening, feeling the music. She watched the musicians in their concentration, she stared at the first violinist's intricate braid.

What was her life like? Did she have a family at home, did her husband come to listen to her perform? Did her kids get to hear her practicing?

At one point, a piano raised from the floor, and a young pianist came out and bowed before taking his seat. He played from memory, bobbing his head with every note, the blond curls on his head dancing with the music.

So much passion, so much talent from everyone involved. Mia was mesmerized.

It ended with a lively, magnificent song, and Mia clapped her hands numb, feeling triumphant not only for Tchaikovsky, but for every artist and performer who had ever risked the shame of failure.

"Did you like it?" Jacob asked, his eyes searching hers.

"I loved it!" she yelled, as clapping and cheers drowned her out. She realized her eyes were filling with tears and she turned away.

"Me too," he said, gently brushing her hand with his.

Late again, they made a mad dash to get back to Lake Union to meet up with Joey. They got to the lake faster than expected, then stood watching the sky in the darkness, scanning for the lights of his plane. He splashed down and pulled up to the dock right on time.

Joey popped the door open. "Hop on, you crazy kids."

Mia, still giddy, hurried after Jacob until she suddenly felt a pull and cried out. Her heel caught in the dock and she toppled forward.

Jacob turned at the last second and caught her, both of them falling.

The world spun around her head, over and over. She'd landed on his chest, his arms catching her before she fell over the side of the dock and into the cold water. He was so close to falling in, his shoulder hanging over the edge.

Their faces were nearly touching. Breath escaped from her chest. She stared into his eyes.

He leaned forward and Mia closed her eyes, a gasp waiting on her lips.

But no lips touched hers.

Instead, Jacob slowly sat up, lifting her effortlessly. "Are you okay?"

Thank goodness for the darkness. Maybe he hadn't seen her close her eyes.

Her cheeks burned red. "I am. Are you?"

"I'm fine. Just glad we didn't fall overboard there."

Joey laughed. "Nice catch. You almost pulled a Russell. I don't need two waterlogged passengers."

She rushed to her feet and forced a laugh. "And I don't need to ruin Bailey Jo's dress."

. . .

It was the music. It had gone to her head. And running through the night with Jacob, the cold air burning her lungs, the promise of a starry late-night flight over the ocean. The glow in Jacob's eyes when he talked about his mom, the warm grin he had when they'd stood for the standing ovation...

All these elements, blended up and served into her already jumbled mind, led to Mia shutting her eyes and waiting to be kissed like that.

What a fool. She could hardly sleep that night. How could she think, even for a split second, Jacob wanted to kiss *her*? He was so obviously in love with Annie, a wonderful person who had known and loved his family for years. Known *him* for years!

Mia was a stranger – someone who kept asking him to break the rules for her – and he kept saying no.

To add more bad news, she awoke to a voicemail from her agent confirming she had a batch of interviews the following week she had to attend.

"You're not going to weasel out of this one!" he said with a cackling laugh.

Mia walked downstairs that morning bleary-eyed, her hair plastered to the back of her head in an unflattering nest.

"Rough night?" Russell asked, pouring a mug of coffee and pushing it toward her.

Mia grunted.

"Is everything okay?" asked Sheila.

"It's fine. I have to do interviews for the movie next week and I'm dreading it."

Russell nodded. "That is part of the business, unfortunately."

"My album is coming out next month, and I've been able to get by with only doing one interview. It was lovely," Sheila said with a smile. "I met with a record store owner who runs a radio station."

"Lucky," Mia said with a groan. "I have to meet with some YouTuber who likes to challenge his guests to pudding-eating competitions and bikini wrestling."

Russell frowned. "Bikini wrestling?"

Mia waved a hand. "Don't worry, Dad. I made sure I wouldn't have to do that. At least not this time." She sighed. "It's so embarrassing to go out and do interviews when there's a chance this movie could be a huge, mortifying flop like the last one."

"You can't worry about how audiences will take it," Russell said. "The real question is how much you loved it. How much did you love making it?"

She shrugged. Love wasn't part of the equation. Only panic. "I have no idea."

"Here's a way to think of it," he continued. "What if you never gain critical acclaim? If you never reach the top of your field and are always subject to some amount of ridicule—would you still want to be an actress?"

Mia groaned. "I don't know, Dad. That sounds awful."

Sheila laughed. "Yeah, Russell, way to sell it."

"It's a thought exercise," he said, putting his hands up. "I don't mean that you'll never be successful. It's a way to understand what you value. Is it the process or is it the outcome? And if you don't –"

Mia put a hand up. "I get it. I just...I have enough to think about right now."

A text popped up from Jacob. "Hope you're not too sore from your fall, and I hope it didn't spoil your night! PS - saw a report that the resident orca pods were spotted nearby."

The shame she'd been picking at all night melted slightly with his warm words.

Maybe he hadn't seen her puckering her lips at him like an ugly stepsister after all.

She picked up her phone and typed a response. "I'm fine. I hope I didn't hurt you! That's great news. Where can I see them? And when can you see Lottie?"

Sheila leaned in. "I'm guessing you're not texting about your interview."

"No." Mia laughed and hit send. "Dad, I'm going to bring Jacob around to see Lottie, if that's all right."

"Of course! The more the merrier."

The weight she'd bashed into her chest all night was gone. It seems she hadn't ruined her friendship with Jacob over her silliness. She wouldn't make that mistake again.

Sixteen

Days after the symphony, Jacob still heard the music every time he closed his eyes. Mia was there, too, her face flashing in snippets – grinning over rice cakes in an amber glow; light glinting in her eyes when they stood to clap and cheer; her figure illuminated by cool moonlight as they ran down the dock.

He couldn't close his eyes without seeing her.

"There's really nothing you want to tell me about the entire evening out?" Annie asked. "Nothing funny? Interesting? Romantic?"

Jacob turned the car into the daycare parking lot. The twins were in the back squealing, both in a jolly mood.

"There's nothing to tell," he lied. "We went to dinner and listened to music. It was fun."

"Fun," Annie repeated. She crossed her arms over her chest. "You're being weird about this."

He pulled into a parking spot and stopped the car. "No, you're being weird. You wanted me to take Mia, so I did. It was fine, and now it's over."

"Margie told me Mia offered to take you to the sea pen site."

He kept his stare fixed straight ahead.

Margie. He should've known better than to tell her anything, but when he had gotten home that night, she was waiting with a cup of tea and a plate of biscuits.

A trap.

Jacob opened his car door and sighed. "I don't know why you're being so pushy about this."

"Because sometimes, Jacob, you need to be pushed." Annie snapped open her door and stepped out of the car.

He followed. He neither wanted nor needed to be pushed. Why did they think they were helping him? Of course he was enchanted by Mia. She was a charming, intelligent, and tenacious starlet.

Emphasis on the starlet. Her new movie was coming out in a few weeks. No matter how much fun they had, no matter how many ways he'd seen her stunning face illuminated, she would soon move on to bigger and better things. She would forget he existed. She'd forget her time on little San Juan Island and the little people that lived their lives there.

For him, it'd be something he could tell his grandchildren. He'd gone out with an actress once, before she was really famous. Wasn't that funny?

He paused. He'd have to remarry to have grandchildren. That wasn't going to happen.

"Hello, little lion!" he said, unbuckling Leon from his car seat.

The twins would be the ones who would have to hear about it, then. He'd bore them with that story in fifteen years. They could be the ones to groan and roll their eyes.

They carried the twins in to daycare, and Annie wasn't able to nag him anymore. Noel didn't want to let go of her. Leon took off like a rocket as soon as Jacob set him down.

He was watching him crawl off when his phone buzzed in his pocket—his boss.

Jacob waved a goodbye and ducked out of the classroom. "Hello?"

"Hi, Jacob. Is now a good time to talk? I've got Mindy from HR on the line."

He unlocked the car and took a seat. "Sure. Is everything okay?"

"I don't come bearing good news. I've enjoyed working with you, but the company is doing some restructuring and your position has been eliminated."

A laugh escaped him. "What? Is this a joke?"

"Your access has been revoked. We'll overnight a box for you to return your computer and supplies. Mindy can go over some of the details of your severance."

"Severance?" He blinked once, twice, three times.

Across the parking lot, Annie's face appeared outside of the building. A smile formed, then slipped, replaced by a furrowed brow.

She mouthed, "What's wrong?"

He shook his head, his mind flooding with foam. "Am I getting laid off right now?"

"I'm going to let Mindy take it from here," his boss said.

A woman's soothing voice came on the line. "Hi, Jacob. This is Mindy. I know these conversations can be difficult, so I am going to be transparent with you."

There was nothing transparent about an ambush like this. "Okay."

"Know this decision hasn't been made lightly. There have been ongoing concerns with your performance, and we've determined the requirements of the role are not aligned with the outcomes necessary for your role during your tenure."

Annie appeared at his window, her forehead wrinkled, a frown fully formed. Jacob held up a finger, indicating for her to wait, and she nodded.

"I'm sorry, what?" he asked. "I thought I was doing well."

"This is about a fit for a role," Mindy said. "It is not personal. You'll receive your final paycheck next week. You're not eligible for severance, and while I understand that can be disappointing, you are eligible for COBRA health insurance and will be receiving that information in the mail."

Her voice grew distant. Jacob leaned over to unlock Annie's door. She slipped into her seat and waited silently until he ended the call.

"What's going on?" Annie asked.

The phone dropped into his lap with a thud. "I just got fired."

Annie gasped, both hands covering her mouth. "Why?"

"I don't know."

He started the car. Of course, he knew why. Or at least, he had a suspicion. "I'll drop you off at work and try to figure out what happened."

There was nothing but road noise, then Annie's quiet voice. "Do you think it's because you've been doing daycare drop offs and pickups? Maybe they're upset with you missing work?"

Jacob shook his head. "Definitely not. Please don't think that. They said it was my performance, but my boss *just* gave me those symphony tickets to show me how appreciated I was."

She turned to him. "Really?"

"Yeah. Something else is going on."

He dropped Annie off, once again assuring her this had nothing to do with her or the twins.

The smart thing to do was to go home. Not to act on the pounding in his chest or the fire in his blood. Make a cup of tea, maybe.

Then again, he knew where to get tea.

Jacob got back on the road. It wasn't far. If Mia was at the tea shop, she could tell him what she'd done. She must have done *something* to get him fired so swiftly. He needed to assess the damage. Would he be blacklisted from every company, or only the ones in the US? He wasn't going to go back to Australia. Ireland seemed nice, if they'd have him.

He got to the tea shop quickly and pushed the door open. Orange and cinnamon filled the air. There were two tables occupied, and Eliza was at the front, selling cookies to a customer.

Mia was off to the side. Her face lit with a smile when she spotted him, and she stood, taking a step toward him. "Hey, stranger!"

"I need to talk to you in private."

"Oh. Okay." She turned, motioning for him to follow.

They walked through a swinging door and into a small kitchen. Teacups were stacked around them, and tins of tea lined the walls. A white kettle dinged, blowing steam into the air.

Jacob stood across from her. "I need to know if you did anything with Ronan."

Her eyes grew round. "Not with Ronan exactly, no. I filed a complaint with the SEC, though."

"What did you say?"

"That I had concerns about Quantum Extend being a Ponzi scheme and I needed to talk about it with someone." She paused. "I called and left a few voicemails, too. Because no one got back to me."

He shut his eyes. That was it. That was all it took. One person at the SEC with dreams of working for Ronan someday went running to him and blabbed it all.

"What's wrong?" she asked.

"I got fired." He sighed. "I guess that explains why."

Mia gasped. "I'm so sorry, Jacob. I didn't say anything about you."

"You didn't have to. I'm the one who introduced you to Ronan."

She looked down. "I may have emailed him, too."

"You *what?* Why would you do that?"

"I wanted to follow up. Flatter him, get him to talk to me."

Heat flashed through his body, sweat springing at his neck.

Jacob shook his head and turned. "Unbelievable."

She grabbed him by the arm. "Wait! I don't see how they would connect any of this to you."

"Of course you don't," he said, his voice rising. "You think everyone is playing by the rules. You don't know what you're dealing with. You don't know *who* you're dealing with. I keep telling you this, but you refuse to hear it."

The kitchen door opened and Eliza stood, frozen. "I'm sorry. I need to grab some tea."

"No, I'm sorry," Jacob said. "I'm leaving."

He brushed past Eliza, past waiting patrons, and through the front door.

He made it all the way to his car before the regret caught up, a cold bucket of water washing over him.

He shut his eyes, once again seeing Mia's face, this time her eyes as round as a frightened cat.

There was no way of knowing if Mia was actually at fault. He knew this, but he'd wanted someone to blame.

He opened the car door and got out again, squinting at the slim figure moving against the backdrop of the blue sea.

Seventeen

"Wait!"

Mia stopped and turned. Jacob jogged toward her, stopping a few feet short.

His cheeks were flushed red, and his hair was tousled by the wind. "I'm sorry."

A lone seabird floated above. If she looked up, it would surely poop on her. That was the kind of day she was having. "No, I'm sorry. The last thing I wanted to do was cause trouble for you, and that's exactly what I did. I'm really, really sorry."

He shook his head. "It's – I'm not..." He sighed. "It was unfair of me to lash out at you."

It wasn't. He'd called it from the first minute she'd had this idea. Mia just couldn't believe it could be so ridiculous – that a man running a multi-million-dollar company could be so petty.

How wrong she'd been. "Are you only saying that because you're afraid I'll try to fix it?"

He cracked a smile. "Yes, that's what it is."

"Well, don't worry," she said. "I'm done with all of it."

He looked down, then back at her, his face creased. "The thing is, you're not wrong. It probably is some kind of scheme. It's admirable you want to help your friend, but..."

"But I don't have a chance," she said.

"It's not you. No one has a chance. How long did Bernie Madoff have his Ponzi scheme going? Decades, right?"

Mia nodded. "Yeah, but –"

"I know, Bailey Jo is in trouble now. I get it. I admire you for trying, but..." he sighed. "I'm sorry, okay? Can you forget what I said?"

Mia had poked and poked until something happened. It just wasn't what she'd wanted to happen.

The damage was done.

She could forget the words he said, sure, but the look on his face would be seared into her foolish little heart for eternity. "Of course. Don't worry about it."

They stood, two pillars, the wind whipping between them.

"I'd better get going," she said. "Joey is flying me to the airport."

He cleared his throat. "Are you taking a trip?"

He might as well be on another planet. His voice sounded so far away, the world he lived in so different than hers. Hers, filled with gossip and reviews and overpriced dresses. His, the real world, where diapers needed to be changed and the powerful ruled from the shadows.

How had it taken her so long to admit it? Her world was a joke.

She nodded. "LA for a week or so. I've got a few interviews and some other errands to run."

Better not to mention that there was a regional SEC office in LA she had wanted to stop by.

"Right. Well, good luck."

She forced a smile. "Thanks."

They split, walking opposite directions.

The house was, thankfully, empty when she got back. She sat on the couch and stared out the window.

There was no point in going to the SEC office. Jacob was right. Ronan did as he pleased. No one was going to stand against him. That was the reason for all the secrecy, all the fear, all the boot-licking. People laid themselves down in front of him, and why? Because he was rich and ruthless.

Mia needed to keep her head down. She wasn't educated in finance. She didn't know all the terms, she didn't know the tricks. Her silly little world involved interviews and dress fittings. That's where she belonged, trying to look pretty.

She would stay away from the SEC office. She'd done enough.

. . .

Getting to LA was uneventful. Her mom was out of town filming, but she had insisted Mia stay at her house. Her mansion.

Fabio picked her up from the airport and took her straight to the stylist, gossiping the entire time.

His voice blended into the wind. "I'm sure you heard they wouldn't even speak to each other at Sundance," and "I saw her shoe collection in Vanity Fair. Wasn't that wild?"

Mia had no idea what he was talking about, but she nodded and made non-committal noises. It was enough.

The stylist was kind, but rushed. She was her mom's stylist, and she'd only agreed to see Mia as a favor.

"Your mom wanted to coordinate your dresses for the premiere," she said wearily. "I have two of her prime picks here."

Mia nodded. "Whatever you think is best."

"She's wearing an emerald green gown. I can show you a picture..."

Mia wasn't sure how it would coordinate, but her mom's favorite pick for Mia was a light gold, shimmery gown with a disappearing neckline and gems cascading down her back.

It was stunning. Mia stood in the mirror and marveled at the sparkle under the lowered lights. "I love it."

The stylist pursed her lips. "It's a little tight."

"I'm guessing you don't have a bigger size."

She raised an eyebrow. "It's couture."

"I'll make sure it fits. And I'll make sure not to do any squats and rip it."

The stylist did not laugh. "I have a few things for your interviews, too."

"Thanks."

After being dressed essentially by her mom, Mia did two short radio interviews and a longer podcast roundtable discussing the movie.

By the end of the night, she was glad she had at least found words to describe the movie. Stepping out of her place of fear, she did love the movie they'd created. She loved the message, and she hoped it would reach the people who needed to see it.

Her performance still left question marks, but the truth was, she believed in the movie. A lot of people, people other than her, had put their hearts into it. It was like the symphony, except the most visible collaborators were the actors, and the other stupendously skilled artists were behind the scenes.

She appreciated that part of it. It was beautiful. It was the rest that scared her.

Luckily, she was exhausted. She got to her mom's house and collapsed into the guest bed.

The next morning, there were three more radio interviews and one with a movie critic. Then she got dressed in a new outfit and filmed the TV interview. It was mercifully short, only twelve minutes, and Mia thought she'd managed not to embarrass herself.

That night, she camped in front of the TV, debating if she could watch it. The six-bedroom house was empty and still. It was too strange to enjoy the pool by herself. Dark and echoey.

She decided to watch an episode of *I Love Lucy*.

A text popped up. Jacob. "Caught you on the Big Night Show. Very cool! Congratulations. The movie looks like it's going to be great!"

She grabbed her phone, her heart racing. Maybe he wouldn't despise her forever? "Was it okay? I couldn't watch it. I go into a fugue state during interviews."

"A very cool fugue state. You seemed totally natural. I'd never guess it made you nervous."

She smiled. "Thank you. That's really nice. Any news on jobs?"

"Not yet. I've applied to a bunch. Not worried about it."

He was probably just being nice – but maybe he was telling the truth. What would it be like not to be in a constant state of panic about work?

"I want to put out some feelers as well," she wrote back. Then she risked it. "Do you still want to check out the sea pen?"

He responded instantly. "I'd love to. I'm free...all the time."

She groaned. "Ouch. That's right."

"Just kidding!" He sent a smile. "But do me a favor. Don't stop by the SEC while you're in LA."

She gasped. How had he known? Had she told him and forgotten?

Or did he have her pegged *that* well?

"Don't worry. I won't. They don't want to see me anyway."

The interviews were over. Jacob was speaking to her. It was better than she could've hoped for.

Now all she needed to do was survive the premiere.

Eighteen

As if his outburst hadn't been embarrassing enough, Jacob proved to be even more of an overreacting fool when he landed an interview within a week of his firing, and got a job offer a week after that.

The company wasn't somewhere he'd want to stay long-term – it was a cloud company serving investment funds, of all things – but it would pay the bills and let him stay on-island to help Annie as long as she needed.

He accepted the job and then set about on the more difficult task: finding a way to apologize to Mia.

The root of a good apology was understanding, but Jacob was too ashamed to fully examine why he'd acted out. It was unlike him; he didn't have much of a temper and didn't normally let things ruffle him.

Why did he let being fired from a job he didn't even like throw him off like that? Not only throw him off – but look for someone to blame.

Was it the divorce, leaving his nerves frayed and his thoughts unkind? Was he getting bitter and cruel in his old age? He replayed his performance at the tea shop again and again, his chest filling with a thick and heavy shame.

He couldn't talk to Annie about it. She was delusional, and her teasing was endless. She'd declare his overreaction was a sign of his passionate love for Mia.

That wasn't it. He knew his place; he wasn't a complete idiot. While she was in LA, running from interview to interview, he sat on his dad's couch, watching her late-night debut on a too-small TV screen.

Seeing her was surreal. Mia walked out and waved to the crowd and flashed her stunning smile to cheers. She had on a black strapless dress, her hair cascading elegantly over her shoulder, and she floated to her seat in five inch heels. He thought the heels she'd worn on their date were impressive, but these were another feat entirely.

Not a date. It wasn't a date. He had to keep telling himself that. They went to the symphony and ran under the stars and almost fell into the ocean, but it was not a date.

How many times had he wanted to reach out and grab her hand...

Jacob was only human, and it was easy to forget Mia was a star when they were laughing over rice cakes. When he spoke, she listened – really listened – without rushing, without questioning.

He wanted to tell himself it was acting, that she couldn't possibly be that genuine, but he knew it wasn't true. She really was the most remarkable woman he'd ever met.

She'd forget him. He knew that.

He was still going to apologize, even if he couldn't fully sort through his jumbled thoughts.

On Saturday, she'd invited him for a flight out to the sea pen to see Lottie. Before he headed over, he stopped in town to find inspiration for an apology gift.

His first thought was flowers, but that quickly unraveled. What kind was he supposed to buy? A bouquet, or a potted plant? It seemed desperate to show up with roses, and all the other bunches looked half-dead.

The potted plants were no better, and Mia wouldn't thank him for getting an overly sensitive plant whose life she had to maintain while she jetted around the world.

A box of chocolates was too Valentine's Day, and a basket of fruit seemed absurd. Who needed that many pears?

He could get a card and write out how he felt, but that would involve knowing how he felt.

Scratch that.

He wandered into the grocery store and stopped at the bakery section. The glass case called to him, filled with colorful cakes, shining donuts, and cupcakes topped with stiff frosting.

Mia didn't need any of this. She had Patty and Eliza to bake for her. She wouldn't be impressed by a box of donuts.

He turned and something caught his eye. A round, flat, chocolate chip cookie cake. It was a foot and a half in diameter with pink frosting lining the edges.

Mia loved cookies...

The baker, a white hat atop his head, nodded a hello. "Can I help you?"

Jacob pointed at the cookie cake. "Would you be able to write something on that for me?"

"Sure. Whatever you'd like."

He grinned. "Great."

. . .

This time, Russell opened the door.

"Jacob!" he said, "Come on in."

"Hi, Mr. Westwood. It's nice to meet you."

"Call me Russell, please." He waved a hand. "It's nice to meet you, too. Mia has tried to keep me from embarrassing her, but she's finally slipped up."

Jacob laughed. Easy charm ran in the family. "I appreciate you letting me take a look at the sea pen site, and Lottie. I find the entire project amazing."

"Of course." He nodded at the bakery box. "Is that for me?"

"Ah, it's something for Mia –"

Russell took the box and slid it onto the kitchen island. "Hopefully she'll share."

Her voice boomed from the top of the stairs. "Dad!"

"Yes, dear?"

She came running down, cheeks pink and hair flying behind her. "Don't harass Jacob."

Oh, to be a family of world-class actors and still have the same problems as everyone else.

Russell put his hands up. "I'm not!"

"He's not." Jacob tore his eyes away from her and picked up the bakery box. "I got you something."

She smiled, eyebrows scrunching together. "For me? Why?"

She pulled the box toward herself and popped the lid open. Her eyes scanned the cookie and a laugh burst out of her.

Russell leaned over her shoulder and let out a singular, "Ha!"

"'Sorry for Overreacting When Everything Turned Out Okay'," she read aloud. Her eyes shined at him. "I don't think it was an overreaction. I got you fired."

Russell looked at Jacob, eyebrows raised. "Is that right?"

"I'm not so sure about it," Jacob said, "and besides, I already got a new job."

"I *am* sure about it," Mia said, putting the box down and pulling out a knife. "It was my fault. This is too kind."

"Sounds like you don't deserve all of that for yourself," Russell said, edging in. "Cut me a part with extra frosting."

She rolled her eyes. "Sure thing, Dad. Anything else you need?"

"I'd take a glass of milk."

She glared at him

Russell laughed. "Kidding. That'll be good for now."

She served him a pizza-sized cut with a stern look. "Enjoy."

Russell winked and took the plate with him as he disappeared upstairs.

"Sorry about him," Mia said, shaking her head.

"You know, I have a dad of my own," Jacob said. "I'm familiar with the art of the dad joke."

"Your dad is a beloved island treasure."

Jacob shrugged. "Your dad is a beloved Hollywood icon."

She laughed. "Beloved. That's something." She picked up the knife again. "Would you like some?"

"Sure."

She cut another large slice, then a tiny sliver for herself. "This isn't personal," she said, sliding a plate towards him. "But my mom's stylist told me I needed to fit into the dress they'd picked out for the premiere, and I'm supposed to lose some weight." She sighed, breaking a tiny piece off the cookie cake. "Cookies aren't part of the program."

"What?" Jacob frowned. "That's absurd. Why are they picking dresses that are too small to begin with?"

A smile spread across Mia's face. "I hadn't thought of it like that. I don't know."

"I know this probably means a lot coming from me," he said, "but I think they're insane to tell you to lose weight."

"Thanks." She looked up at him and scrunched her nose. "That's kind."

He felt bad eating this in front of her. He took a small bite of the cookie. The chocolate was a perfect balance to the chewy sweetness.

"I'm sorry it's so big, then." He made a face. "It had to be to fit my long message. I wanted to add more, but the baker was already annoyed with me."

She laughed. "Don't be sorry about any of it. This is perfect. Chocolate chip is my favorite."

"I thought so."

"What's this new job?" she asked.

"Nothing exciting," he said with a wave. "Cloud maintenance for a place that has investment clients."

"The cloud," she said, smiling down at her plate. "You know how much I like messing with the cloud."

"I do." He laughed, finishing off the rest of his cookie. No need to drag it out. "Anyway, I am genuinely sorry about what I said and how I behaved. I was way out of line, and though you don't have to believe me, I don't normally blame others for my failures. I'm really sorry."

She popped the last bite of her cookie sliver into her mouth and shook her head. "I have that effect on people. The SEC won't even talk to me."

"Really?"

She nodded. "Yeah. I've turned myself into a real nuisance over the last few weeks, playing pretend reporter."

"You do it with style," Jacob said. "You'd make a great reporter."

She stopped. "Do you think so?"

"I do." He paused. "Though you obviously have another lucrative career. I'm not saying you should change jobs, but –"

"No, I take that as a compliment," she said, beaming. "I've always thought that was such a cool job. I had a friend in high school, Katie, who went on to be a reporter. I admire her so much."

"Oh yeah? What kind of stuff does she do?"

"Everything – financial crime, coverups, corruption. She was always really into journalism at school, even going after the school board. She broke a story about embezzlement by one of the school's contractors."

"Wow."

Mia nodded. "I know. She's always been a serious person, and a renegade."

"You're a renegade."

She looked down at her empty plate. "I wish."

Before he could find the words to tell her he meant it, Mia walked toward the door and picked a pair of dark sunglasses from a shelf. "Shall we?"

Maybe it was best he kept his admiration to himself. "I can't wait."

She smiled. "Me too."

Nineteen

One foot in front of the other, all the way to the dock.

Mia kept her head down and counted her steps. If she could get to a hundred, she could focus her thoughts. Fifteen, sixteen, seventeen…

Jacob's face when he brought that cookie cake. That *smile.*

Maybe she could have a slice later. It seemed like he wasn't mad anymore. He could forgive her, she wouldn't be deprived of his jokes and his calm smile, and…

Whoops. One, two, three, four…

The cookie itself had been so soft and chewy, with just the right amount of chocolate chips. She had half a mind to run back into the house and eat the entire thing right now. The tiny movie premiere dress could stuff it. She'd borrow something from Bailey Jo.

Jacob didn't think she needed to cut out cookies – clearly, since he'd bought her a giant one.

She should eat the entire thing.

Mia looked up. The sky shined blue with a few wisps of clouds. They were nearly to the dock. She could focus for a few seconds.

Birds called out overhead, and a small spout of air erupted near Joey – a seal? The seals seemed to like Joey. Perhaps he had an understanding with them. Eat, float, and be merry.

She glanced at Jacob. He was squinting, his eyes focused ahead. The last time they'd been on a dock, she'd fallen onto him. He caught her so gently in those big arms...

No, no! Eyes down, counting steps. One, two, three, four...

An image of the cookie cake floated into her head. She'd never had the urge to eat the entirety of one of those before, but that was the problem with limiting food. It immediately made her want to overeat to an unreasonable degree.

That was probably all it was with Jacob, too. She knew he was taken, that his heart belonged to another, and it drove her mad. The flutter in her chest wasn't real. The dreams of his laughs and his eyes weren't caused by anything genuine – only driven by the fact that she couldn't have him.

She'd never done this before – fallen in love with a taken man. It wasn't her style, but there was a first time for everything. It didn't mean she would do anything about it.

Yet she'd invited him out on the boat. She knew he couldn't resist seeing Lottie, and she couldn't resist seeing him again.

Joey stood, waving. "I just heard they're taking Lottie on a walk today! They said you can come."

"How do you walk a killer whale?" Jacob asked, a bemused smile on his face. His eyes were focused on the water.

Mia looked down. She needed to watch her step. She couldn't very well excuse falling into him again. "I haven't gone, but my dad told me about it. They take the boat out, get her out of the sea pen, and go into the open ocean. She swims alongside. It helps her build her stamina."

"It's not like she has a leash, though, right?" Jacob asked. "She could swim off into the sea, never to return?"

There was true alarm in his voice.

Mia smiled at him. "Theoretically, yes, but she's well-trained. Beyond that, she's not stupid. She's a cautious whale."

"A cautious whale. I guess I never thought much about how different personalities might play out."

Mia nodded. "For a while she lived with a reckless male orca, and he was always trying to get into things he shouldn't. He stole a trainer's cell phone and snatched seagulls off the surface of the water."

"Snatched seagulls?" Joey said, eyes wide. "To eat?"

Mia got into her seat and pulled on her headset. "Sort of. He hunted them, made a game of it. He'd put a bit of fish at the top of the water as bait, then stay there until they touched the water. Then bam! Snap them up."

"That's incredible." Jacob shook his head. "But Lottie didn't do stuff like that?"

"No. She liked to surprise people and blow bubbles. She's much sweeter. The male orca would purposely lure people close and splash them. Sometimes he'd poo in the water first."

Joey made a face. "Ew!"

Mia shrugged. "Don't hate the player, hate the game."

"The male didn't like being gawked at," Jacob said. "He didn't want to be a star, and he took the matter into his own... fins."

A laugh burst out of her. "Jacob, you get it."

They made the short trip to Stuart Island, Joey hogging the conversation the entire way, pointing out the different islands to Jacob and offering bits of history.

"If you ever get sick of this gig," Mia said, "you can open your own island tour company."

Joey turned around, his mouth hanging open. "Why didn't I think of that?"

"You should probably get a helicopter license, too," Mia said. "To vary the experience."

"I've wanted an excuse to get my helicopter pilot license for years." Joey shook his head. "Mia, you're a visionary."

If only she could envision any sort of future for herself. It was much easier to think of other people. Her future was like staring into an underwater cave.

Dark, airless, hopeless.

Okay, that was dramatic. But she felt very alone.

They landed, and Joey walked them to the trainers' quarters. "I'd go with you, but I have to pick someone up from Seattle."

"Thanks for the ride," Mia said.

"Any time!"

Joey disappeared, and Jacob turned to her. "I like him."

Mia smiled. "Me too."

Lottie's trainers, Sue and Terry, walked in. Mia introduced everyone, and Sue took the lead.

"Lottie's been working on her distances, so today we'll see how far she wants to go," Sue said.

"Sometimes we don't get far," Terry added. "She finds a particular kelp forest that interests her, or a group of fish, and then she wants to watch them for a while."

Adorable. Much more adorable than her poo-splashing tank mate – though Mia still felt like she could relate to him.

"I really appreciate you bringing me along," Jacob said. "I'll make sure to stay out of the way."

Terry waved a hand. "It's a pleasure to have you both. Let's go!"

They walked out to the boat. Jacob and Mia boarded, then found a spot to huddle together in the back. It took a few minutes to get Lottie out of the sea pen, but then they were off, with Lottie's sleek figure breaking the water behind them, then appearing next to them, causing cheers from Mia and Jacob wherever she popped up.

"I'm always blown away by how big orcas are up close," Jacob said, eyes fixed on Lottie breaking the water with a small leap. "Whoa!"

Water sprayed his sunglasses and he turned to Mia, grinning.

She flashed a smile. "I know. I thought this boat was big, then she shows up next to it and it feels like a child's toy."

"Exactly. She could flip it if she felt like it."

"Thankfully, she's more interested in kelp forests!"

They continued north, into the Strait of Georgia. Lottie kept up with the boat, frolicking in the wake. She was so big that when she slammed down, she rocked the boat with her waves.

"I forgot to ask if you get seasick," Mia said, laughing as water splashed into her face.

"Thankfully, I don't." Jacob grinned. "My sister does, and she always has to take something. She'd probably be asleep right now, then really upset she was missing everything."

They were cruising along when the engine fell silent.

"Is everything okay?" Mia asked.

Sue turned, her face wide with a smile. "Yeah, everything's fine. Great, actually. We got a report that orcas are headed our way."

"Who is it?" Jacob asked. "Residents or transients?"

Lottie's family were resident orcas – that is, the ones who ate salmon, not mammals.

"Residents," Sue said. She shot a glance at Terry. "It might be Lottie's mom."

Mia gasped. "Is this the first time they'd be seeing each other again? Since Lottie got out of the park?"

"Yes. The first time in decades." Sue bit her lip, eyes scanning the horizon. "They could change direction at any time, though. Right now, they were spotted swimming close to the shore, so we'll stay here and see what happens."

Mia turned. Jacob had his eyes on her and her heart leapt.

"I have a good feeling about this," he said. "I could always tell when we were going to see the orcas and when we weren't."

"An orca sixth sense?"

He nodded. "You can feel it in the air. Don't you feel that?"

"Uh huh." She laughed and looked down. She felt something in the air – her own delusions, crowding out any sort of intuition Jacob was tapping into.

The trainers busied themselves with Lottie, instructing her to swim out and back repeatedly, then rewarding her with fish.

Mia and Jacob hung back so as not to distract them. Watching Lottie's slow, precise movements in the water was mesmerizing. How could an animal so large be so graceful?

They were waiting for Lottie to surface on the other side of the boat and touch a target when she disappeared beneath the water and swam off.

"Do you think she heard something?" Mia asked.

"She might have," Terry said. "Our hydrophones aren't picking anything up, though." He paused, clutching headphones to his ears. "Wait. Just there. I hear them."

"What if it's not Lottie's family?" Mia asked in a low voice. "Will they hurt her?"

Jacob shook his head. "The different orcas pass each other all the time. They seem to have a policy where they don't interact. The residents and the transients don't even speak the same dialect, so it's easy enough to ignore each other."

"That's incredible." Mia peered over the edge of the boat. "I don't want Lottie to get hurt."

"She won't." Jacob bumped her with his shoulder. "These are her people, so to speak."

Of course he'd know all about orcas. Why wouldn't he? He was an island dreamboat of a man, all rugged and ship-wise and orca-smart.

The trainers kept calling to Lottie, using whistles and their voices. Ten minutes came and went without sign of her.

"She's never done anything like this," Sue, scanning the water with binoculars. "I'm starting to get worried."

Terry stepped forward. "Don't be. I'm sure that –"

A spout of air blasted ten feet away. It was Lottie, spy hopping with her head out of the water. Not fifteen feet behind her, blows exploded from the water.

Within seconds, they had completely surrounded the boat. Black fins broke the surface. Orcas leapt, slamming into the water while others slapped the water with their tails.

It was a celebration.

Mia's chest tingled. She couldn't breathe out, her head spinning. Jacob caught her as she stumbled back into a seat.

"Are you okay?"

"Yes." She put a hand to her chest. "I can't believe this."

Terry and Sue let out whoops and hugged. "Lottie found her. She found her mom!" Tears streamed down Sue's face.

Jacob's hand was warm and dry, still holding Mia's. "Are you sure you're okay?" he asked.

Mia's mouth hung open and a laugh escaped her, releasing the pressure. "I think I'm in shock."

The orca party carried on, complete with jumps and loud whistles and clicks. They sat and watched for half an hour.

"We're finally able to get Lottie's attention again, so we're going to try to move," Terry said. "I don't want Lottie to get too tired to get back home." He started the boat and they slowly started moving.

Luckily, Lottie followed – as did the other orcas, all the way back to the sea pen. They got Lottie back inside, and her mother stayed outside the nets, calling to her.

"I'm not sure what protocol is here," Sue said, grinning. "Do we let the whole pod have a sleepover?"

"I don't think you have much of a choice," Jacob said with a laugh.

"You're welcome to come back tomorrow and see what's going on," Terry said. "This is really unprecedented."

Mia's heart sunk. "I would love to, but I'm going to be out of town."

The movie premiere. It was only a few days away, and she had to do a fire round of interviews beforehand. At least this time, she got to do them with her mom, but still. There was no backing out, even for a once-in-a-lifetime whale event.

"Thank you so much for taking us out today. That was the experience of a lifetime," Jacob said, shaking Terry and Sue's hands.

Joey flew them back to San Juan Island and they said their goodbyes. Mia's dad wasn't home, so she sat in the darkness of her room as the silence overcame her.

Thoughts swirled, swift and desperate. She texted her mom. "What do you think of me bringing a date to the premiere?"

"Not a great idea," she wrote back. "You need to keep the focus on your career."

Mia didn't respond. She crept downstairs, picked up the cookie cake, and ate it all before falling asleep.

Twenty

After their magical trip out on the water, Mia disappeared. Whisked off to LA for the press tour and the premiere, taking control of the life she was meant to live.

At night, alone with the glow of his phone, Jacob flipped through the pictures they'd taken together. Lottie leaping in the boat's wake. Sun on the water and blurs of black on the horizon. Mia leaning into him for a selfie, a grin on her face, the reflection of his outstretched arm in their sunglasses.

Try as they might, they couldn't get a picture with both them and a whale in the background. Twelve attempts, twelve failures. By the end they had both been laughing hysterically, their heads filling the crooked frame.

He couldn't think of a reason to delete any of them.

The week pushed him past his limits. First, the critics' reviews of the movie came out. He read every one, agreeing heartily with the reviewer who called Mia "a revelation," and taking personal offense to the one who said she was "a pretty prop."

What did he know? Jacob looked up everything about the guy. Talk about failures. He'd tried to direct movies of his own decades ago, all of them flops. Now he was an expert?

That was the only critical one, really, and it was still positive overall. Audiences loved the movie. One woman wrote that Mia felt "like a best friend who knows all of my secrets."

His chest swelled when he read that. Mia's earnestness must come across on screen, and people could tell. That was really her.

He had to see it for himself. The movie was small, with a limited release, and the nearest theater that was showing the movie was in Seattle. He booked a flight for the weekend.

Despite his intentions to stop obsessing over the movie then, it was too hard to resist listening to her interviews. He let himself listen to each one *once*. Plus, he had to see the pictures of her at the premiere to make sure she'd found a dress to wear.

She had, and she looked stunning. She was a star.

After much debate, Jacob sent her a carefully worded text at week's end.

"Congratulations on the movie! So excited for you and your huge success – you've earned it!"

"Thank you!! It's been a whirlwind," she wrote back.

After several drafts, he sent a half-joking response. "Can't wait for you to get the movie screened here on the island."

"That's a great idea! I will totally do that, and you'll have to tell me if you like it."

He grinned down at his phone. "I'm sure I will."

An hour later, his phone dinged. He rushed to grab it, his heart sinking when he saw who it was from.

Not Mia. Caroline, his ex-wife, asking about their old home insurance policy.

The day before, she'd texted asking about a recipe he used to make. The week prior, a cartoon about a koala and a kookaburra.

It was odd behavior from Caroline. They'd spoken occasionally since the divorce, but not this much, and not on such friendly terms. She was almost acting like nothing had happened and they were still jolly friends.

He didn't know what to make of it. He mentioned it to Annie, and after studying the messages, she declared, "Caroline's lonely." She handed the phone back. "How does it make you feel?"

He paused before answering. "Nervous."

The night before flying out for his secret screening of Mia's movie, he stopped at Annie's to help with bedtime. After they had the twins asleep, Annie told him about her updated theory.

"I think Caroline saw this," Annie said, pulling up a news story on her phone. The headline read **MIA WESTWOOD: NEW MOVIE AND NEW MYSTERY MAN?**

Jacob's mouth dropped open. It was a picture, paparazzi-style, of him and Mia crossing the street the night they'd gone to the symphony. They were laughing, Mia tumbling into him in her high heels.

"I'm betting Caroline can't stand to see you moving on," Annie said. "That's why she's texting you, bothering you."

Jacob couldn't stop looking at the picture. Mia looked so happy. They'd had a nice time, hadn't they? It was gone now, but it was real. "Might be."

"Doesn't that annoy you?"

He sighed and rubbed his face with his hands. "It's how Caroline is. I wouldn't read too much into it. Whatever it is, it'll pass."

She tended to do things like this. Hop from one idea to the other, sure she'd know what she wanted once she'd found it.

He'd learned a lot about Caroline when they were together. Just not enough to make her happy.

Before getting married, they used to live down the street from Caroline's sister and her husband. They'd had two kids, a boy and a girl. Caroline loved her niece and nephew.

She and Jacob were always over, helping with the kids, and that was when Jacob became a baby expert.

Not only babies, but the toddlers too. He found the age so charming. The way toddlers see the world was so interesting, and so much about human nature was revealed in their raw takes on life – their wonder and awe at bubbles, clouds, and airplanes. The infamous toddler rage at seemingly innocuous things like the wrong color milk cup and an incorrectly peeled banana.

Jacob thought people were exaggerating when they talked about toddler rage, but it was real. Throw-down, kicking-and-screaming-on-the-grocery-store-floor real.

Caroline's two-year-old nephew could go from joyous kisses to a meltdown in seconds. But unlike adults who threw tantrums, he'd recover in minutes like nothing had happened.

And, unlike adults with tantrums, his fury was understandable. He was only three feet tall, people misunderstood half of what he tried to say, and he had no power over anything.

Jacob learned everything from that little guy. The most absurd tantrums were when he'd request something, Jacob would give him *exactly* what he'd wanted – a blue water cup, the bunny crackers, his red hat – only for fury to erupt on his little face.

"No!" he'd scream. "Green cup!"

It took a while for Jacob to understand it, but it was the picture of human nature. The little guy realized he was unhappy, asked for something he thought would improve his situation and, after getting exactly what he wanted, still felt unhappy.

Cue rage.

It made perfect sense. How many times had Jacob gotten what he'd wanted, what he'd wished for, only to feel disappointment? That was life, wasn't it? Life was disappointing.

It had taught him a lot about Caroline, too. If only *she* had been able to understand it, maybe their lives would have gone a different way. Maybe she would have stopped looking outside of herself for all the answers.

"When are you going to see Mia again?" Annie asked.

Jacob snapped out of his memories. He shrugged. "I don't know. She's going to be busy after this."

"Well, I think –"

Jacob cut her off. "When are you going to see Roy again?"

She rolled her eyes. "Roy said he'd come for the party, so I guess then."

"Has he said anything about work? Is he done with whatever project he was working on?"

"It should be finishing up in a week or two, yeah."

Jacob stared at her. "And?"

"And," Annie said slowly, "I don't know. He hasn't talked about moving back yet. He hasn't suggested we move out there, either, or said anything about a formal custody agreement." She shrugged. "Sometimes I worry the twins and I don't fit into his life anymore."

"How can that be?" Jacob shook his head. "You three *are* his life."

"I don't know, Jacob. I wish I did, but I don't."

He sat back in the couch. He shouldn't pry, but how could he not say anything? He'd talk to Roy and get his side of the story at the birthday party. There had to be something missing, some sort of breakdown in communication between the two of them.

Roy wasn't a bad guy. He was behaving in an incredibly boneheaded way, but he couldn't possibly intend to lose his family. Jacob was sure of it, and seeing everyone as overgrown toddlers who had never learned to control their emotions or communicate was helpful in identifying problems.

There had to be something, some deep toddler impulse, keeping him from behaving rationally. Maybe Jacob could do some good and figure it out, or at least point them to a couple's counselor.

"I, for one, am excited for the party," he said.

Annie's eyes darted toward him, a half-smile on her face. "I hope you bring Mia."

He groaned. "You never give up, do you?"

"Never." She grinned. "Not in a million years."

Twenty-one

After the interviews, after peeling off the too-tight dress, the blinding flash of cameras, and the squealing giddiness with her mom – after all of it, Mia was back in the tea shop, sitting on a tufted pillow in the Japanese-themed tearoom across from Bailey Jo.

"I can't wait to see the movie," Bailey Jo said. "I'm so proud of you."

Mia looked down. Patty had insisted they use one of her special tea sets today: white bone China brushed with delicate pink roses. It was one of the most beautiful things Mia had ever seen.

"Thank you," she said.

"What's wrong?" Bailey Jo tilted her head. "Did something happen at the premiere?"

"Not with the movie, no. That was all fine. It was great, actually." She let out a breath. "I've been so worried that it would be another flop and I'd embarrassed myself, but...I didn't plan for what's happening. I didn't put any thought into the chance it could be a success."

Bailey Jo set down her teacup. "I know what you mean. Sometimes success is harder to handle than failure."

"Yeah, why is that?"

She sat back, narrowing her eyes at the ceiling. "You reach a goal – whatever it is – that you thought would make you happy, but that's not how life works. There's no mountain you can climb where you're suddenly fulfilled. You get to the peak and realize you're still...you. For better or for worse."

"Wherever you go, there you are," Mia said with a smile.

Bailey Jo downed the rest of her tea. "Yup."

"I'll figure it out," Mia said. "I need some time away to process everything. I'm a slow processor."

"I get it. I am, too," Bailey Jo said.

"And I'm really sorry I haven't been able to find anything to help your case. I'm still waiting on a response from the SEC, though."

"That's kind of you." Bailey Jo leaned back, her eyes drifting to the ceiling. "My lawyer is upbeat, but I don't have high hopes."

Eliza popped in and took a seat. "Whew, sorry. I got a little too involved in a new Victoria sponge recipe. What did I miss?"

"Just musings on life," Bailey Jo said with a sigh. "Sad, sad life."

"Oh dear." Eliza poured herself a cup of tea. "We're going to need more tea."

"I haven't been able to help Bailey Jo, despite my best pathetic efforts," Mia said. "All I've managed to do is get Jacob fired."

Bailey Jo's mouth popped open. "Really? What happened?"

"He was the one who introduced me to Ronan, and after I started poking around, Jacob's boss went from giving him gifts of appreciation to an impromptu phone call with HR to tell him his performance was poor and they were letting him go."

Eliza winced. "Getting fired like that is such a shock to the system."

"Wow." Bailey Jo shook her head. "That's awful, but I'm not surprised."

Mia set her teacup down. "I seem to be the only one who was surprised by it. I'm so naïve."

"Don't think of it that way," Bailey Jo said. "You're honest, and honest people often assume other people are honest, too. To their peril."

Eliza laughed. "Bailey Jo, can I please get you something to lift your mood? A cookie? A flower? A hug?"

Bailey Jo raised her eyebrows. "I could go for a hug."

She stood and Eliza followed, pulling her in tightly and patting her on the back. "I'm sorry things are so tough right now."

Bailey Jo patted her back. "Thank you. It's nice to be able to complain."

"Complaint club," Mia said, tilting her head. "You don't hear enough about those. We should start one."

"I think we have," Bailey Jo said.

"Hello, girls!" a voice called out.

Mia looked up. Margie's face smiled down at her. "Hi, Margie!"

She stood and Margie hugged her, then Eliza and Bailey Jo.

"Wow, two hugs in one day," Bailey Jo said through laughter. "Why doesn't my lawyer do this?"

"Because then he'd have to bill you for it, and he's probably not very good at it," Margie said. She turned to Mia and grabbed her hands. "Congratulations on your movie! I've heard wonderful things. I can't wait to see it."

The smile on her face was more genuine than all the congratulations she'd gotten in LA last week. There were a few people who had gushed, seemingly over-the-top, about the film. Others laced their comments with an edge of disdain.

Was it jealousy? Mia could never tell. It just made her want to run.

"Thank you, Margie," Mia said. "I'm going to get a screening here on the island."

"Yes, Jacob told me!" She clapped her hands together. "I can't wait. I'm going to bring my book club."

"I don't mean to be rude," Bailey Jo said, "but I realized I have a call with my attorney in a few minutes. I'll see you ladies later."

"Take care," Margie said. She let out a puff of air and put her hands on her hips. "Have you seen Patty? She was going to help me set up for the twins' birthday party."

Mia looked over her shoulder. "I haven't seen her all day."

"Oh," Eliza said slowly, "She told me she threw her back out this morning."

"Is she okay?" Mia asked. "I can go check on her."

"I'm sure she's fine," Margie said, waving a hand.

Eliza cleared her throat. "I can help set things up after I close the shop."

"I can cover the tea shop if you need," Mia said. "I don't mind."

"Well..." Margie's eyes darted to Eliza, then back to Mia. "Did I tell you Eliza is making special sugar cookies for the party? Shaped like hot air balloons, clouds, and little presents!"

"Yum!" Mia paused. That sounded like a lot of work, actually. "Er, if you're busy, Eliza, I can help Margie set up."

A smile flashed across Margie's face. "That would be wonderful! Are you busy right now?"

There was nothing for her to do the rest of the day except wade through existential dread, and there'd be plenty of time for that when she was staring up at her ceiling later that night.

"Not at all," she said. "Lead the way!"

• • •

Margie offered to drive and Mia accepted, getting the details of the party on the way over.

"I was able to borrow an enormous ball pit from a friend of mine who runs a daycare," Margie said. "The bouncy house will be set up tomorrow. The petting zoo will be here for the older kids, and those who are kids at heart."

"You're a dream party coordinator," Mia said.

Margie turned to her with a grin. "That's so nice of you to say! I don't often get to do children's parties, because my children have yet to bless me with grandkids, and it's been such fun planning this party."

"You love your job, and it shows," Mia said.

"I love making people happy."

"Hm." Mia paused. "That's what my mom always says about her movies. They make people happy."

Margie's eyes grew wide. "I *love* your mom's movies! She's right—she brings a lot of joy to a lot of people."

Was that something to latch onto? Would Mia's latest movie make someone happy, make someone feel seen?

She could try to hang onto that for later. For now, she tucked the thought away.

They pulled up to the house and got out of the car. "I just need a few finishing touches around the house," Margie said. "Jacob can tell you what needs to be done outside. Thanks so much for your help!"

She spotted him against the backdrop of the grand barn. Her heart jumped into her throat.

"Mia!" A smile spread across his face. He walked toward her, closing the distance quickly. "Fancy seeing you here."

"And you!" she said, a stupid smile on her face. "Margie recruited me to help set up."

"Oh. Lucky us."

Lucky her. "I've been meaning to tell you – Lottie's family has been visiting her at the sea pen every day."

He set a box down and shook his head. "Incredible. Just incredible."

Before she could stop herself, she added, "We'll have to go back to see them again soon."

"I would love that."

A woman with brown hair and blue-green eyes stepped out of the barn. Her eyes danced between them, a smile on her lips.

"Mia, this is Annie," Jacob said, jerking a shoulder.

"Hi!" She stuck a hand out. "I'm Mia Westwood."

"It's so nice to finally meet you!" she said, shaking hard. "Jacob's told me so much about you."

Mia shot a glance at him. "You mean how I got him fired?"

"Oh, that?" Annie waved a hand. "That was nothing."

Mia laughed. "Right."

"It wasn't her," Jacob added. "It was my poor performance."

So that was what he was going with. He was, as ever, a saint.

Mia went on. "I've heard so many things about you, too. I don't know if Jacob passed on the message, but I am desperate to babysit your kids."

Annie laughed. "He did pass it on, and thank you. He's always trying to get me out of the house."

"All she wants to do is sleep," Jacob rolled his eyes. "She's too irresponsible to sleep at night like a normal person."

Annie narrowed her eyes at him. "You'd better watch it, Kowalski."

A knot lodged itself in Mia's throat.

They were cute together. Incredibly cute. It wasn't just Jacob, either. Annie was adorable, too.

A smile froze on Mia's face and the air turned to ice in her chest.

Jacob scoffed. "Yeah, yeah."

"I better go inside and make sure the twins didn't over-power Hank," Annie said. "Thanks for your help! Please, please be sure to come tomorrow. It's going to be a beautiful day!"

"Oh, ah – thank you!" Mia said.

Annie smiled and disappeared into the house.

Mia turned to Jacob. "She's lovely."

"The best, honestly."

Mia's heart pounded in her ears. Her hands were ice, her breaths shallow. "You two are very cute together."

He stopped. "Thanks?" Jacob narrowed his eyes. "Oh, we're not – Annie and I aren't a couple."

"Right," Mia rushed, adding, "I know she and her husband are separated, but –"

Jacob laughed, cutting her off. "No. She's like a sister to me."

Heat splattered through her veins and filled her chest. "Oh, I just assumed – I'm sorry!"

He stared at her for a beat, then flashed a smile. "It's fine. I'm sure everyone suspects it." He laughed. "But no, she's like my little sister. I'm actually going to have a talk with her husband Roy tomorrow."

Could it be true? She hadn't allowed herself to even consider the possibility. If his heart wasn't promised to Annie...

Mia raised her eyebrows. "A talk?"

"Yeah. See what he's thinking." Jacob shook his head. "I don't get it. He's all but disappeared on her, and he's not like that. The two of them love each other. They've been together for a decade, and they both love those kids."

"That's so incredibly sad."

"It is, and I know Roy's been a bonehead. From what Annie told me, he had a sort of breakdown. I get it. It happens." He sighed. "He can't give up on a love like that."

She smiled. "True love conquers all, eh?"

"Don't look at me like that," he said, grinning. "But yes, it does. It always does."

"Good to know." Mia cleared her throat. "Okay. Am I supposed to be doing something?"

He laughed. "Yes. You are. We need to set up two temporary fences. There are going to be so many kids at the party, Margie wants to be sure we've fenced off the play area so no one wanders down to the water."

Mia nodded. "Good thought."

"She also wants to keep the petting zoo animals from invading the barn. It's for people only. Go figure."

A laugh burst out of her. The air stung her lungs as she gulped it back.

Try to play it cool. Try to build this fence and not think about what he said until later. Build the fence.

She could build a fence. Probably.

She could do anything if Jacob wasn't in love with someone else. Her heart soared, her head spun. Jacob handed her a roll of wooden fencing, and she held herself steady as she raised her arm to accept it.

He set about pounding posts into the ground with a mallet.

"We'll put these about six feet apart," Jacob said between blows, "and string the fence part up with these hooks."

My, his biceps really showed with that mallet.

Mia forced herself to focus on connecting the first pieces of the fence. Once she had a section strung up, she stood back and squinted.

"This is going to be much more aesthetically pleasing than I'd expected," Mia said. "Margie has a touch."

Jacob nodded. "She does."

"How's your new job treating you?" she asked. "I hope it's not too awful. I still feel bad."

Jacob shrugged, a half-smile on his face. "You're going to have to let that go. They pay me more, and the work is easier. I can't complain."

"It's not the sort of work you want to do, is it?"

"No. I've always wanted to work for a company that does something important – puts something good into the world, you know? Maybe bringing clean water to people or installing solar panels. I don't know." He laughed. "Now I'm stuck tending the cloud for a bunch of investment gambling junkies."

"Aren't we all," she said with a sigh.

He stopped swinging and wiped his brow with the back of his hand. "Indeed. Wise words."

She grinned. "Thanks. I try."

The peace of the birdsong and the sea broke with the sound of a car bumping up the driveway.

Jacob stopped and put a hand over his eyes, blocking the sun. "Any idea who that could be?"

Mia shook her head. "Nope."

The car stopped. A pair of long, tan legs extended out of the driver's seat. A woman hopped out, her sun-kissed brown hair cascading down her shoulders in waves.

"Jacob! Guess who!" She called out, her voice rounded with a beautiful Australian accent. "I've made it!"

Twenty-two

"Caroline?"

Jacob stepped back. The fence post in his arm clattered to the ground.

"Surprise!" she yelled.

Caroline strode toward him, sliding a pair of sunglasses to the top of her head. Her hair was longer than the last time he'd seen her, but everything else looked the same. Her piercing hazel eyes, her bright white smile.

"San Juan Island." She shook her head. "Took me long enough, eh?"

He blinked. His brain was rubber. "How did you find me?"

Not the most clever question in the world, but it was the first one to pop out.

"I stopped by the police station on my way in. Everyone was as friendly as can be. They gave me directions." She stopped short of him, her arms at her sides. "You look well."

"I can't believe you're here," he said.

"Well, believe it." She smiled again, her eyes drifting toward Mia. "Hello there! Look at you, you're even prettier in person."

Jacob missed Mia's reaction. His eyes were stuck on the apparition who looked and sounded like his ex-wife.

"Thank you!" Mia said, her voice quiet. "I think I'll see how Annie's doing."

She walked toward the house and through the front door. Jacob stared at the shut door, the white paint blinding in the daylight sun.

"You have no idea how happy I am to see you," Caroline said.

He snapped his eyes back to her. "Caroline, what's going on? Why are you here?"

"Can't a girl come for a visit?"

He stooped to pick up the fence post. "When it involves an eighteen-hour flight, not really."

She sighed. "I wanted to tell you I was coming, but every time I tried to find the words..."

Her voice cracked.

Jacob stopped. "What happened?"

"It's my dad. He was doing so well..." Tears flashed into her eyes. "I lost him, Jacob."

A punch landed in his gut.

Caroline's dad had been the quintessential Australian man. Always kind and gregarious, always welcoming. Jacob loved him. His health struggles began just before Caroline started pulling away from their marriage.

"I'm so sorry, Caroline."

Tears spilled onto her cheeks, launching to the ground. A sob retched from her.

He pulled her in to his chest. "I'm sorry."

She sucked in jagged breaths. "I don't know what I'm doing here, Jacob. I'm a mess. I didn't know where else to go. I haven't been able to stop thinking about you. I didn't know who else to turn to."

"It's okay." He broke the hug and stood back, looking at her. "You know I always loved your dad."

"Yeah." Caroline wiped a hand across her cheek. A smile flashed across her face. "Not as much as he loved you. He was so mad at me about the divorce…" She shook her head. "When he got sick, I think I lost my head. I don't know. I don't know what I've been doing for the last year."

He hadn't noticed it looking at her, but she was thin. Her bones had pressed into him when he held her. Her grip was weak. He could probably pick her up and carry her away.

"My sister has her kids and family. I have nothing."

"That's not true," he said.

She shook her head. "I needed to see you. I don't expect anything, and I'm not asking anything of you. I just needed to see someone who loved him like I did. I needed to go somewhere before I completely lost myself. So…I bought a plane ticket."

"You love a spontaneous trip," Jacob said.

She looked up at him. "Is this okay? Me being here?"

He could feel her trembling in his arms. "Of course. You're welcome here, and you're not alone, okay?"

She wiped tears from her cheek and pulled away. "Thanks, Jacob."

Twenty-three

True love conquers all. That was Jacob's mantra, wasn't it?

She breathed in as Margie's living room spun around her. Mia braced herself against the couch, then lowered herself to the floor next to Noel.

A wooden puzzle lay between them. Noel thoughtfully picked up a flat, wooden circle and tried to fit it into a too-small slot. Leon stood a few feet away, hanging on to the couch and staring with pouted lips.

"I'm not here to cause trouble, Leon," Mia said, shaking her head.

His scowl broke into an open mouth grin to reveal tiny square teeth.

"Was that funny?" Mia smiled and shook her head again, this time more vigorously, her hair bouncing wildly around her face.

Leon's mouth opened, laughing, and he shook his half-bald baby head back at her.

"I can do this all day." Mia leaned forward, shaking and shaking to Leon's laughter.

The room kept spinning, but at least it broke him from his suspicion. Still clinging to the couch, he stomped his chubby legs toward her, squealing as he fell into her arms.

"You are going to be walking in no time, aren't you?" she asked.

He put a hand on her cheek, then pushed her chin out.

Mia laughed, shaking her head again. He squealed.

All the while, Noel kept her focus on the puzzle. The largest circle perplexed her. She had tried it in every opening until finally reaching the largest spot. It slotted into place, and Noel sat back and clapped her hands.

Mia kept her voice low. "Look at that! It fits!"

Noel turned to her, beaming. Leon put both of his hands on Mia's face, trying to force her head to move. Mia laughed and obliged.

Even with all the ruckus they were making, Mia couldn't block what was happening in the kitchen. Margie and Annie were pressed against the window, murmuring to one another in low tones.

Mia couldn't make out most of what they were saying, but she clearly heard Margie exclaim, "*Why* is he hugging her?"

Why indeed.

Mia didn't have to ask. She knew. She saw the astonishment on Jacob's face when Caroline had appeared, the look of longing in her eyes.

Lovers reunited. It was exactly what Jacob had imagined for Annie, except he was getting it himself.

Mia's short-lived dream was shot dead, right in front of that beautiful barn by the sea. She'd long suspected Jacob's heart was locked up, promised to another, and for that glorious half an hour, under the sun and with the ocean breeze filling her chest with hope, Mia thought it might be her.

How could she have been so blind? That was why he kept bringing up his past with Caroline. Jacob had made it clear, in his polite way, that his heart was elsewhere.

What an airhead she was.

No, not even an airhead. A pretty prop. That was what one of the movie reviewers had called her. He loved the movie and said the only downside was Mia. "She's a pretty prop and nothing more."

The words were seared into her mind, painful because they were true.

She had no business being in that movie – or in any movie. She brought no substance to it; she brought no substance to anything!

Her attempts to help Bailey Jo were useless. Worse than useless where Jacob was concerned – she'd damaged his career. How could she think he'd have any warm feelings for her after that?

She'd pathetically fallen in love with him anyway, and when the love of his life had walked back into the picture, she'd seen what Mia was instantly.

"You're even prettier in person," Caroline said, smiling, totally genuine, because Mia was an empty threat.

Pretty, empty, vapid. That was Mia.

"Is everything going okay in here?" Annie asked.

Mia jumped. She hadn't heard her come in. "Everything's great," Mia said. "Leon is debating how soon he should take his first steps, and Noel is solving the mysteries of the puzzle universe."

Annie smiled. "Thanks for keeping an eye on them. I got a bit distracted."

"Honestly, it's my pleasure." Mia smiled. "They're a welcoming pair."

"Leon is usually wary and less than welcoming," Annie said. "But it looks like he's decided to climb all over you, so what do I know?"

"He can't resist my charms. And by charms, I mean my hair." Mia paused, locking eyes with Leon.

He stared back at her, his cheeks round and serious. She smiled, then quickly shook her head back and forth, her hair flying as Leon erupted into laughter.

"That's pretty much all it takes," Mia said.

"Aw!" Annie laughed. "You figured out the secret, then."

"I guess so."

Margie's voice erupted from the kitchen. "I'm not going to keep hiding in here. If she won't come in and introduce herself, then I'm going to have to introduce myself."

"Give them a minute," Hank said.

"They've had several minutes!" Margie said. "That woman should know Jacob is not a toy she can pick up and put down when she –"

Hank cut her off. "I'm not saying I disagree with you, but he's an adult."

"The fact he's an adult doesn't mean he doesn't need us!" Margie said.

"I'm not saying he doesn't need us," Hank said gently. "But we have to let him sort it out. It's his life."

Margie let out a harumph.

Mia caught Annie's eye, then looked at the twins. Leon was staring at her, and Noel was watching with a bemused smile on her face.

Who was Mia to keep the crowd waiting? She shook her hair, both twins breaking into giggles.

"I'm missing all the fun in here," Margie said, stepping into the room.

Poor Margie, trying to put on a polite face. Mia would make her exit and hopefully never have to see Jacob or any of them again.

Since Margie had driven her, though, she was trapped for the moment. She'd walk home if she had to, trudging through the grass as cars whizzed by.

"I should get going," Mia announced, standing up. "It was nice seeing you all."

"Do you need a ride?" Hank asked, leaning against the doorway. "I'm going into town."

"Why do you need to go into town at a time like this?" Margie snapped.

A smile tugged at his lips. "I was going to get those streamers you wanted."

She crossed her arms. "Oh. That's right."

Mia flashed a smile. "Bye-bye, Leon. Bye-bye, Noel! Happy birthday to you both!"

Annie rushed to her feet. "Thanks so much for your help today."

"I barely did anything," Mia said waving a hand, "but you are welcome."

Annie's stare was unbroken. "No. Thank you. Really."

"I hope you can make it tomorrow," Margie said.

"Oh." Mia's eyes flashed between Annie and Margie. They were both staring at her, smiling. Margie's smile was especially wide. "You don't have to invite me, it's –"

"Nonsense!" Margie put an arm around her. "You can't miss it. I ordered too much food. Patty and Eliza will surely stay. Bring Sheila and your dad, too! Everyone is welcome. It's going to be a wonderful day."

Mia forced a smile. "It sounds like it'll be a blast –"

Margie cut her off. "Good! We'll see you tomorrow."

Hank shot her what she thought might have been a pitying smile. "Ready to go?"

Mia nodded. "Yes. Thanks for the ride."

They made their escape, getting to Hank's truck without being seen, and he mercifully didn't talk about anything except the tides until they got back to her dad's house.

Twenty-four

What a mess. An hour ago, Annie had thought Margie was a genius. She had tricked Mia into coming over and forced Jacob to see what he was missing with his own two eyes.

It was captivating. Annie had craned her neck in the window, watching them. They were clearly in love! Smiling like fools and making twinkly eyes at each other!

Most obviously, Jacob was happy again, re-engaged with life. Mia, though inexplicably shy, clearly adored him. How could he not see it?

Maybe Margie still was a genius. Her plan would've worked were it not for Caroline appearing out of nowhere.

No one could have predicted that. It was a meteor falling out of the sky and onto their heads. Even Mia seemed rattled by it. Annie had to fight the urge to hug her when she'd found her sitting on the floor.

The twins' birthday party was supposed to be a chance for all of them to have a fresh start – Annie, Roy, the twins, and especially Jacob. Caroline's arrival felt like a dark omen.

"I don't know who she thinks she is," Margie growled. "You don't get to divorce someone, then show up out of the blue and start hugging them!"

Annie peered out the window. Jacob hammered in a post while Caroline strung up a stretch of fence. She stopped to say something to him and he laughed, wiping his brow.

She sighed. "If you're Jacob's ex-wife, you do."

"How can he let her waltz in here like this?" Margie said. "She already broke his heart. How many more chances does she want?"

"For Caroline..." Annie trailed off. "As many as she can get."

Margie spun around, her face red, her lips pursed. "I won't allow it!"

"She's not a bad person," Annie said slowly. "She doesn't hurt Jacob on purpose."

"It doesn't matter *why* she does it, she still does it," Margie said.

"I know; I'm just saying. I think it makes it harder for Jacob. He obviously still cares about her, but he knows what she's like."

"And what exactly is she like?" Margie asked, hands on her hips.

Nothing Annie could say would calm Margie down, and truth be told, Annie wasn't feeling charitable to Caroline right now either. "She's confused. That's the simplest way to put it."

"I'll give her something to be confused about," Margie said, her hand on the doorknob.

Annie grabbed her shoulder. "Don't. If you go out there when you're angry, you'll say something you regret."

"I'm not angry. I'm livid! I can hardly see straight." Margie picked up a rag, wiped the counter, then threw it over her shoulder. "Jacob came here to recover from what she did to him. He came home."

"I know."

"And she shows up at his home? Wanting what now? What else could she possibly want from him?"

Annie turned to face the window. "I don't know."

She wouldn't say it to Margie, but there was a chance Caroline wasn't confused at all. Perhaps she'd finally realized leaving Jacob was a huge mistake.

Like it or not, that was a happy ending. That was what Annie was waiting for when she laid in her bed late at night, wondering when Roy might have that same epiphany.

Two months and still nothing. They talked. She sent pictures, he updated her on work. He checked in on the twins, came to visit, took them out.

Yet there were no long conversations between Annie and Roy, no late-night chats. He apologized for being away, but there was no depth to his words. No sudden clarity that made him realize all he was missing out on, no desperation to get back to the little family they'd created.

The days ticked by and an uneasiness grew in Annie's chest. It was as if Roy were getting more comfortable being away with each passing night. More comfortable in a new life that didn't include her or the kids, except peripherally, like they were people he sent postcards to.

It felt like she didn't know him anymore. Maybe he didn't know himself.

Margie stormed back and forth across the kitchen. "What am I supposed to do with myself?"

Annie couldn't judge what was happening between Jacob and Caroline. It wasn't her business. She could hardly handle her own life. How could she give advice to anyone else?

"You can help me put the twins down for their nap," Annie said.

Margie looked down and sighed. "That would help me feel better. Maybe you'll let me hold Leon for his nap. I know it's not a good habit, but –"

As if Annie had the luxury of demanding good habits from her twins. Noel preferred her independence, but Leon always accepted – demanded, even – endless cuddling.

"Leon would love it. And if it would make you feel better..."

"It would." She scooped him off the floor. "Come here, little one."

Annie watched as Margie carried Leon down the hallway.

How red-hot was Margie's fury with Roy? She kept it well hidden. Annie had never heard a cross word, but she could imagine.

It was comforting to know people were upset on her behalf, but it was as helpful as a kiss she planted on one of the twins' boo-boos.

Ultimately, she and Roy had to heal the wound in their marriage. No one else could do it for them.

It was the same with Jacob and Caroline. No one else could interfere. He was outside, blissfully unaware of the conversations going on behind closed doors.

Annie's heart hung heavy in her chest. The twins' birthday would be a turning point for her, one way or another. Waiting was exhausting. As filled with dread as she was, at least she'd get some answers.

She scooped Noel into her arms. "Come, my little darling. It's time for a break."

Twenty-five

The twins' party ballooned to over sixty guests, growing into an impromptu family reunion for Annie.

Jacob was glad for it. Cars pulled up to the house and entire families piled out, all smiles and shrieks and brightly colored wrapping paper. It was the best party he'd been to that year – all joy, no pretense.

He stood on the driveway with his dad, guiding cars into spots. Caroline volunteered to direct the groups toward the barn and show them where to unload gifts.

"Since I'm an uninvited guest," she reasoned, "I think it's best if I act like an extra party planner. Stay out of the way. Maybe get me a headset? It's less awkward than explaining who I am."

He wasn't going to argue with her. Whatever she needed to do to stop bursting into tears was fine with him, but he suspected her behavior only added to Margie's frosty treatment – not that Caroline noticed. She wasn't aware of Margie's normally overwhelming warmth, and thought even her frosty level of warmth was too kind.

Jacob's way of dealing with everything was to keep pretending nothing was happening. He kept introductions short, and neither his dad nor Margie asked any questions – which was good, because he didn't have any answers.

"It looks like we've got most of the guests here," Hank said, standing back and scanning the cars. "I'll help any stragglers if you want to head into the party."

There was still one group notably missing, unless they'd snuck in and he'd missed an entire car. Not a sign of Eliza or Patty...

Or Mia.

Jacob nodded. "Thanks, Dad. I'll go and see how Annie's doing."

Maybe they'd decided not to come, or they'd only drop in for a minute. Why would Mia waste her day at a children's party? Surely she had more glamorous places to be.

He shook his head. He needed to stop thinking about her. It was lucky she'd stopped by yesterday. He probably would never see her again – not in person.

She had truly been stunning in her latest project. It was clear her path was set – she was The Next Big Thing. He'd happily follow her career from afar, silently cheer her on. The beautiful starlet he was lucky enough to know for one perfect summer. At least they'd had a chance to cross paths, however brief.

If he kept telling himself that, he might believe it one day.

He walked to the barn, a glorious blue sky reigning above them. A honky-tonk version of *Old McDonald* blared over the speakers as a group of kids used the temporary fence as a base for tag. The fake wood strained against the impact but stood tall.

A balloon archway, one side pink, one side blue, cascaded over the gate into the party. Jacob strolled beneath it, dodging a kid whizzing by in hot pursuit of another.

Jacob walked to the nearest fence post and gave it a shake. Perfectly stable, despite the blows. He smiled to himself. Not bad.

The twins were occupied – Leon in the arms of Annie's mom, and Noel being carried by a precocious eleven-year-old cousin of Annie's.

Margie waved him over. "How does everything look?"

"It looks amazing. You do great work, Margie."

She beamed. "Thank you. It seems like everyone's having fun. The petting zoo should arrive in an hour. Do you think there's enough food? Maybe I should put out more..."

"Looks fine to me, but I'll check inside the barn." Jacob said. "Have you seen Annie and Roy?"

Her lips fell into a thin line. "Annie is around here some-where. Roy is in the barn, holding court."

Jacob suppressed a smile. "Thanks."

The towering barn doors stood open. Pairs and trios of adults were inside, chatting and laughing around tables of food. The supplies were plentiful – more than plentiful, flanked with bouquets of flowers that filled the air with an aroma of freshness.

Roy stood in a corner, facing a group of no less than ten people. Jacob didn't recognize him at first. His hair was grown out, no longer the close-cropped style he'd sported for years. It was shaggy, held back with a headband, accented by a puffy beard with shoots of grey running through.

Jacob walked toward the group and Roy paused his storytelling. "Hey man, good to see you!"

"You too." Roy stepped in for a hug. Jacob gave him a pat on the back. "Did you get lost in the wilderness or something?"

Roy laughed, scrubbing a hand to his beard. "Yeah, sort of."

The crowd parted and Caroline's head popped out. "He was telling us about his adventures on Mount Rainier."

There was an edge to her voice. Jacob narrowed his eyes and she smiled at him before turning to face Roy.

"Yeah, where was I?" Roy snapped his fingers. "Oh right, so we're on the side of this mountain. It's pitch black, we have no idea where we are. Our clothes are soaked from the surprise storm, and we're fighting for our lives trying to put up our tents against this insane wind. We finally get them up and spend the night thinking we're going to freeze to death." He shook his head. "We make it to morning, I open my tent and see this."

He pulled out his phone. On the screen was a snow-capped peak glowing in soft golden light, alpine meadows and towering evergreens woven through.

"It was the most beautiful view I've ever seen in my life. I wasn't sure I hadn't died and gone to heaven."

A younger woman, maybe twenty years old, laughed loudly. "That is *so* cool. You're basically living my dream."

Jacob didn't recognize her—probably one of the distant cousins. No one in the family who knew what Roy had been up to could look at him with such adoring eyes.

"When was this?" Jacob asked.

"A month ago. It was insane!" Roy laughed, tucking his phone into his pocket. "Maybe the beard saved me, huh?"

The group laughed. Jacob flexed a smile.

How did Roy have time to step away from work and camp on a mountain when he didn't have time to see his kids?

Caroline caught his eye and raised an eyebrow. They were thinking the same thing.

Jacob looked over his shoulder. Annie wasn't around. It was a good chance for him to figure out what was going on with Roy.

He stepped forward. "Can I talk to you for a minute?"

Roy nodded. "Of course. What's up?"

Jacob led him to the back of the barn near a table of untouched vegetables. "I wanted to see how you're doing with, you know, everything."

"It's been rough." Roy shoved his hands into his pockets. "I'm not going to lie. The separation has been hard."

"I'm sure."

Roy nodded. "Work is back to normal, though. I think I have things under control."

"That's good." Jacob paused.

How did his dad do it? He never asked questions he wasn't supposed to. How did he manage not to pry into things he so badly wanted to know?

Jacob wasn't there yet.

"What about Annie? Have you guys talked?"

"We talk. We talk a lot." He sucked in a breath through his clenched teeth. "Listen, man, I've had a lot of time to think. I love Annie, and I love the kids, but there's a lot of life I'm not willing to miss out on because things have changed."

Jacob tilted his head. "What do you mean?"

"You'll see what I mean if you ever have kids." His eyes drifted up, his mouth open for a moment before speaking again. "It's just different. It's amazing, but it's a shift in your world."

"Yeah..."

Roy went on. "Annie and I used to drive all over the country. We used to be able to pick up anytime and go camping, or fishing, hike up any mountain."

"I know." Jacob nodded. "You almost killed me on that march through the desert."

Roy chuckled. "I'm still sorry about that."

"Water under the bridge."

"I need that in my life, though. It's hard to explain..." He sighed. "I'm not willing to give our lives up the way Annie is."

Jacob blinked. It was as if Roy had spat air into his eyes.

"She's not giving up," Jacob said. "She's adapting to a new life."

"We tried to take the kids for a one-mile hike once. It was a disaster." Roy shook his head. "My whole life I've put other people first. When do I get a turn? How long am I going to put off living the life I want?"

It took everything for Jacob to not sputter out, "When you're not a dad with two small kids?"

Instead, he said, "So what are you thinking?"

Roy shrugged. "Obviously, I need to be with the kids, but Annie has to make room for me to live my life, too. I have to be able to live life on my terms. I can't take care of the kids if I can't take care of myself."

"Uh huh. Self-care."

"Yeah. We need to figure out boundaries, and we need to sort out priorities. I can't throw the life I want away. That's what we're going to figure out, and honestly, I'm excited about it."

This time, Jacob knew he wouldn't be able to stop himself from saying something he'd regret, so he said nothing at all.

"I appreciate you helping her," Roy said. "I really do. We'll figure it out. Don't worry about us."

This was not Roy. This was a decoy who looked like Roy but spouted off things he'd heard on a podcast or read in an indulgent autobiography. He was a space cadet, far off in the stars, leaving them all behind.

Roy walked off, surely to find some young googly-eyed admirer who thought his stories were anything other than self-congratulatory crap.

It was dizzying to try to work through the flawed logic and therapy speak. Self-care? It sounded like selfishness.

Jacob trudged through the barn doors, back to the sunlight. He needed a cleanse after that conversation.

No wonder Annie had been so confused the past few months. Whatever crisis Roy was going through, he wasn't done. He seemed to only be going deeper into it.

Yet what did Annie make of all of this? What choice did she have but to go along with this out of character behavior? How long could Roy act like this before it *became* his character?

Jacob stared at the crowd. Smiling faces, foil balloons swaying against their ties. The gate under the balloon archway opened, and Mia appeared.

Her hair blew slightly in the wind, a neatly wrapped present in her hands. The pink bow matched the dress loosely clinging to her curves.

It was too much at once – Roy, the mountain, the sound of one of the twins crying.

Jacob stepped forward and stumbled, catching himself on a nearby table. Mia caught his eye and raised a hand in a small wave.

He waved back, his heart pounding against his ribs.

Twenty-six

The wind blew Jacob's shirt taut around his muscles and tousled his hair. A half smile danced on his face.

Two thoughts hit her at once. First, Jacob looked dreamier than ever, and second, there was truly something wrong with her.

She couldn't keep doing this. She couldn't keep torturing herself.

Yet here she was.

Mia walked toward him, clutching a present in her sweaty hands. "Hey, Jacob. Do you know where I can put this?"

"Hey! I'll show you." He took the box, giving it a gentle shake. "This is for me, right?"

There was no sign of Caroline. Maybe she'd gone home? "Yes. I know how much you love building blocks."

He laughed. "Finally."

She fell into step alongside him. "The fence looks great. I saw a kid fly into it and it stayed up."

"I've been impressed with it, but I don't know if it can hold all day." He put the present on top of a merry pile and turned to face her. "I'm glad you could make it."

"Of course! I wouldn't miss this for the world."

That was, at least, the truth. It could truly be the last time she could make an excuse to see him. She wasn't going to miss it, no matter how painful it was.

"How's everything going?" she asked.

"Fine." He paused, lowering his voice. "The party is good, but I just spoke to Roy. Honestly, I don't know what is wrong with him."

The wind whipped hair in front of her eyes, and she pushed it away, frowning. "What did he say?"

"He said he wants to get back into the twins' lives."

"That's good," Mia said slowly, "right?"

"Not really. He said it has to be on his terms. He needs self-care to be able to care for them."

"Hm." She pursed her lips. "What does that mean, exactly?"

"He needs more time to sleep on the sides of mountains to become the outdoorsman he was always meant to be."

"I see." She looked down. "He wasn't like this before?"

Jacob shook his head. "He and Annie liked being outdoorsy, but they were a normal couple. Now he's taking it to the extreme. I can't make sense of it. It seems like he's..." He trailed off, wincing.

"Being incredibly selfish?"

Jacob let out a sigh. "Yeah, doesn't it?"

"It took having two kids for him to realize he wanted to live a bachelor's life," Mia said. "I don't think it's that uncommon – for people to lose it like that."

Jacob sighed. "I don't get it."

"At the same time," she added, "whenever I see someone who so adamantly knows what they want, I assume they must be right." She paused. "That's not what I mean. I don't think Roy is right, but that –"

Jacob held up a hand. "I know what you mean. The confidence is confusing."

"Exactly." She paused. "I don't know where people get this confidence. I've been looking for confidence all my life, just to decide where to step."

"It's self-delusion, not self-confidence." He laughed. "And come on, you have to be feeling a little confident. You have a hit film behind you. You can take off and leave this little island behind."

Leon toddled by, both hands held by a woman who looked so much like Annie. It had to be her mom.

Mia's mom told her it would be unwise to have kids before her career was established. "Give it at least five years, maybe ten," she'd said.

"I'm even worse than Roy," Mia said, her voice small. "I don't know what I want. I think I'm just a brat."

"What? No." Jacob shook his head. "Where is this coming from? Is everything okay with you?"

She let out a breath. "Yeah. Don't worry about me."

"No, really." He stared at her. "What's wrong, Mia?"

If this was the last time she was going to see him – for real this time – why not unload her fears? Why not have a last hurrah with his puppy dog eyes?

"I've been obsessed with making this film a success and now...I don't even care about it. I almost feel worse that it was a success. It means I have to do it again."

"No, it doesn't. Just because you're good at something doesn't mean you have to keep doing it."

She wasn't good at it. She'd gotten lucky.

Mia shrugged.

He went on. "Take me, for example. Do you know how many male modeling jobs I had to turn down so I could be a cloud engineer?"

She stared into his eyes, her face cracking into a smile. "I had no idea."

"Yup. It was a lot."

She laughed, shaking her head. "It's not fair. I have all this opportunity. Between my mom and my dad, I have a huge leg up. I can't waste it."

He stepped in front of her, their shoulders squared off. "Mia, you can do anything. If you don't want to be an actress, the more power to you. What would you want to be if you could be anything?"

She rolled her eyes. "You're going to laugh."

"I won't."

"I don't want to say it."

"Whisper it," he said, leaning in.

She laughed. "I think I'd want to be a reporter, but you saw how that went."

"I did. You were the only one who wasn't afraid to stand up to someone powerful."

"Yeah, and it didn't do any good," she said.

"Do not bring up my firing again," he said, holding up a finger. "It showed me how stupid I was being. I was afraid. Everyone is afraid of Ronan – except you. That means something."

She cast her eyes down to her shoes. If only she and Bailey Jo had the same shoe size. She'd never have to shop again. "Thanks, Jacob. That's kind of you to say."

She looked up. His eyes were zeroed in on her. Her breath caught in her throat.

"The animals are here!" Margie's voice boomed over the crowd. "They'll be ready for visitors in fifteen minutes!"

Jacob flashed a smile. "I'd better go. I need to make sure my fence can stand up to a donkey."

"Good luck!"

He walked off, and within seconds, Caroline joined him. He didn't look back.

Mia's heart hissed like a balloon returning to earth.

•   •   •

The rest of the party was perfectly pleasant. The cake was light and airy, the twins were adorable, the farm animals were hilarious – one of the sheep tried to eat Patty's purse – but she didn't get to talk to Jacob again, and that was all she could think about.

He went from reinforcing the fence to gathering wrapping paper into garbage bags to running off to help put the twins down for their naps. All the while, Caroline hovered behind him, handing him things and looking at him adoringly. They worked like a seamless unit, hardly needing to speak.

Worst of all, Patty wanted to stay after to help clean up and chat. Mia thought she'd have no choice but to stay and torture herself more, until she got a text from Bailey Jo.

"Any chance you're free to chat?"

"Yes," Mia wrote back. "Please come and rescue me from this party!"

She'd done enough pining after Jacob. It was the last time she was going to do this to herself. He was back with his one true love, and she would respect that.

She just couldn't keep watching.

Bailey Jo arrived in fifteen minutes. Mia was reaching for the car's door handle when Margie came running after her with a Tupperware container. "Wait! You need to take some cake!"

Mia paused her escape to accept it. "Thank you. It was beautiful, Margie. I know who to go to next time I'm throwing a party."

"Oh stop. You're too sweet." Margie patted her on the shoulder. "You know, I never got to thank you for setting things up. You'll have to come to my house for Sunday dinner next week. It's a famous event, you know."

Mia smiled. "Is it?"

"It is, and you have to let me repay you for your help."

She'd hardly done a thing, and it wasn't wise to keep coming back. Mia was serious about not seeing Jacob again. "Thank you, but –"

Margie held up a hand. "I won't take no for an answer. I will keep inviting you every week until you accept."

This was more a threat than an invitation. What were the chances Jacob would still be around? Caroline surely had a job she had to get back to, and he would follow. He'd been biding his time on San Juan Island. Maybe serving his time, with all Mia put him through.

Mia forced a smile. "In that case, sure."

"Great!"

She got into the car and shut the door before anyone else could get her. Bailey Jo pushed her sunglasses on top of her head and leaned back.

"Girl, you look fabulous. What kind of one-year-old party was this?"

She smiled. "One where I watch the man I'm in love with frolic in the sun with his ex-wife."

Bailey Jo's eyes widened and her eyebrows shot up her forehead. "What! This is Jacob we're talking about?"

"Yeah. They're the perfect couple. I don't know why I do this to myself."

Bailey Jo threw the car in reverse. "Let's get you out of here."

They sat quietly, listening to the sounds of the road.

Mia's thoughts rolled on. "You know," she said, "it's really his fault. I can't help how I feel about him."

"Of course not," Bailey Jo said with a nod.

"The first time I haven't felt like a loser in months was talking to him. That's how he pulls me in."

"Lures you with compliments." Bailey Jo shook her head. "The nerve."

"No, it's not like that." Mia smiled and shook her head. "Maybe I'm too enamored to see it, but he believes in me. He really...sees me."

Bailey Jo's mouth popped open. "I believe in you! I loved your movie."

Mia turned to her, wide-eyed, before looking away.

"What?" Bailey Jo asked. "What's that face?"

"I feel silly saying this to you, because you're so famous. And also because your problems are way bigger than mine –"

"We do not need to compare troubles," Bailey Jo said. "I want to know what's going on with you."

Mia sucked in a breath. "I don't think I want to be an actress. I hate being famous, and I'm not even that famous, and I feel like I have no idea what I'm doing and..."

"What?!" Bailey Jo grinned. "You think I'd encourage you to be famous? No way. It's the worst! Celebrity culture will kill you. Tempt you in every possible way. Feed the ego and turn you into a monster you don't recognize. Was it John Updike?"

She paused, then continued. "Yeah. He was the one who said, 'Celebrity is a mask that eats into the face.'"

Mia laughed. "Wow."

"It's true. You have to love acting more than anything in the world to keep doing it."

More than anything in the world. That simply wasn't the case. If anything, acting was fear-based for her. Fear of missing out on an opportunity. Fear of disappointing her mom. Fear of making nothing of her life. "I see."

"In my case, it's performing that I love more than anything. Even still, sometimes I'm still not sure if I'm cut out for it. I'd never tell anyone to do it, though. Ever. I'm serious."

A compression in her chest released. Mia took a deep breath and laughed. "Why didn't you ever tell me that before?"

"You never asked! I didn't want to scare you away. I didn't want to limit your dreams."

"It's not my dream. It's my mom's." She let out a breath. It was the first time she'd admitted that out loud. "I didn't want to let her down, but I don't think I can do it. I really don't."

"Then don't. Save your sanity, go off and do something else. Anything else." Bailey Jo puffed out her lips. "Before you end up a target for greedy men dragging you through the court of public opinion."

"I'm so sorry this is happening to you. I got a letter from the SEC this week declining to interview me. Can you believe that? Refusing to even talk to me!"

"I believe it," Bailey Jo said. "Ronan is their golden goose. Why would they want to challenge him? Did you see he was on the cover of Forbes?"

Mia groaned. "Yeah. I saw. 'The Next Revolution is Coming to Your 401k.'"

"Barf." Bailey Jo rolled her eyes. "He's a criminal. I can't figure out how to prove it yet."

"I wish I could've helped."

Bailey Jo turned to her and smiled. "You did, just by trying. No one else cared. They think I'm guilty, or they not-so-secretly hope for my demise." She paused. "That's actually the first sign that you'll never be happy famous."

"What is?"

"You weren't actively rooting for me to fail."

Mia laughed. "Guilty."

"Oh! I almost forgot. I have good news. Does Jacob still need a job?"

"He got a new one," Mia said, "but he doesn't love it."

"I have a friend I met through my animal rescue. He's got a new startup where he's doing all kinds of amazing things – making a new app to help find lost pets, building energy-efficient animal shelters. They need a cloud guy."

"Wow. Jacob would love that."

Bailey Jo beamed. "Really? I can put in a good word. They need an honest person."

Mia sighed, her eyes fixed on a hint of the sea between the trees. "He's an honest person."

"Great. I'm going to send you the email later. But, for now, I'm going to take you for a picnic."

It was nice to have friends. Mia sucked in a breath and turned toward her. "Sounds perfect."

Twenty-seven

That week, Jacob's boss asked him to make a trip to the mainland to work on-site for a new client. He said yes, of course, but the timing was less than ideal. Caroline was still staying in a rental in town, and Roy was in the process of moving his stuff back to the island.

The night before he left for Seattle, Jacob invited himself over to Annie's to help her prepare for Roy's return. She was embarrassed at how messy the house had gotten – which was ridiculous, considering she'd been single-handedly taking care of the kids for months – but he kept it to himself.

Caroline tagged along, busying herself with the kitchen while Jacob and Annie sorted through toys in the living room. The twins had gotten so much at their birthday party that some old toys had to go to make room.

"How are you feeling about all this?" Jacob asked.

Annie's eyes stayed down. She lifted her shoulder in the tiniest motion. "Relieved, I guess? Anything is better than being in limbo."

"That's true." Jacob tossed a plastic octopus that neither of the twins ever played with into a box. "Waiting is hard."

"I don't know how it's going to work yet." Annie shut her eyes and ran a hand through her hair. "For the time being, he wants to keep his apartment in Seattle."

"Why?" Jacob asked.

Caroline peeked over from the kitchen, catching Jacob's eyes. Wisely, she stayed silent.

"You know," Annie waved a hand. "He says he might need it for work, or when he needs time to himself."

"What about you having time for yourself?" Jacob snapped.

Annie rolled her eyes. "I don't want time to myself. I want time as a family. I want this nightmare to be over."

It wasn't his place to judge, and it wasn't his place to comment. Annie was having a hard enough time already.

But wow, it was hard to keep quiet.

"I can help with the daycare run and bedtimes while Jacob is away," Caroline said.

Annie turned to her with a tired smile. "I think I'll take you up on that. Thank you."

"Anytime."

At the very least, Roy's leaving had forced Annie to accept help. That was a first for her.

Caroline was having some firsts as well. Jacob had never seen her in such a delicate state. The last thing Caroline ever wanted to be was vulnerable, but it seemed she'd finally met her limit. As nighttime approached, she grew quiet and fragile. One night she fell to pieces over a mug of spilled tea, sopping up the mess with napkins as tears poured down her face.

He felt bad leaving her, and he didn't know how long his work project would take. It largely depended on how quickly he could figure things out. Maybe it was good they'd have each other for the few short days he'd be gone. They got along well enough, and Caroline needed something to distract her from her overwhelming grief.

To Annie's credit, she didn't make any comments about Caroline dropping in. It was a welcome change from Margie's prying eyes and even a few hints his dad had dropped.

For the morning of his trip, he made sure to book the first sea plane into Seattle. From there, he stopped by the office and picked up a company car.

The work was nothing exciting. They needed to deal with an investment company's legacy software, software everyone else was afraid to touch for fear of breaking something. They were moving to a new system, and it was time for the final steps in moving all the data and processes over.

Jacob had been the one selected for the task after his boss yelled with delight when he'd found out how much experience Jacob had with the old program.

"I've been dreading handling this," he'd said. "We need to make sure everything's working and the backups are in place. This company does millions in trades every year."

Jacob smiled. "No pressure, right?"

"Yeah, right." His boss laughed. "They work with Quantum Extend." He dropped his voice to a whisper. "Big deal, you know? They do all their trades."

A chill ran through Jacob's veins, pulsing into his hands. His breathing slowed. "No kidding."

"Their AI stuff is confidential, as I'm sure you know. But I'm sure they won't provide anything you're not allowed to see."

"You got it, boss."

Jacob drove to the building in silence. No music, no podcasts, only the sound of the road and his heavy breathing.

How badly he wanted to call Mia to tell her – but it was confidential, and it could cost him his job. Again.

He couldn't leak company secrets...but he was allowed to look around. Required to, even.

The company lived in a brown building with black frame windows – the most boring place on earth. He wouldn't be surprised if Ronan had never stepped foot inside.

He walked in and wandered to the elevators before finding the right floor. A woman from the IT department met with him and showed him to a workstation.

"I appreciate you coming out," she said. "The previous company we'd hired to transition this for us kept failing. They sent four people here, and every one of them told us they couldn't safely transition the data. We were starting to get worried."

Jacob kept his face neutral. "I'm not planning on leaving until I figure it out."

That was the truth. He logged in and got to work. There were a few notes and records from the previous attempts to move the data off the old system, and it seemed the first part had been completed. The data there contained a small handful of trades totaling less than a million a year. Peanuts for a firm like Quantum Extend.

The notes stopped when it came time to transfer anything having to do with Quantum Extend's top secret AI investments completed by Ronan's proprietary software.

His heart rate quickened, clicking through the code.

It wasn't set up any differently than the previous trades. Why had *four* programmers failed to transfer the data?

Maybe it was because there was so much of it. Thousands of log files from millions of rows of data. The super-secret AI program was inscrutable. No column labels, no numbers that corresponded to things he expected, and nothing he could make sense of.

He spent ten hours that day trying to piece it together, then twelve hours the next, his neck and shoulders stiff and creaking by the end.

Finally, he had his answer. He knew exactly why no other programmers were able to migrate this data.

The data was all nonsense. The AI program spit out junk. Worse than junk, it spit out fake, retrospective trades that were never made. There was no trading, there was no secret.

It was all a lie. One big Ponzi-shaped lie.

Twenty-eight

S he was serious this time. No more hanging around Jacob, even if Margie had cornered her about Sunday dinner.

Mia had a plan. She could put off attending indefinitely – at least until Jacob and Caroline were safely back in Australia.

Her first excuse would be illness, and to plant the seed early, she would use the island gossip network. She told Patty she thought she was coming down with something early in the week. Then, on Saturday, she would text Margie the bad news.

It would've worked perfectly, had Jacob not texted her on Friday. "Hey! Margie said you're coming to dinner on Sunday? I need to talk to you. It's good news."

Mia stared at her phone, her heartbeat in her ears. What could he possibly be talking about?

Stick to the plan. "I'm not feeling so good. Can you text it?"

His response was swift. "I can't put it in writing..."

Right. "Is this a prank?"

He sent back a winking face and nothing more.

That Sunday, she put on her favorite dress and drove to Margie's, cursing herself the entire way.

Annie opened the door. "Mia! You're here!"

"I'm here," she said, forcing a tight-lipped smile.

Annie pulled her in for a hug. "I was worried because I heard you weren't feeling well."

Darn. Her lie would've worked, if only she could've stuck to it. "Yeah. Must've been allergies or something."

Or something.

A man's deep voice shouted, "Leon!"

It wasn't Jacob. It was someone she didn't recognize. Roy?

Annie led her into the house. No sign of Jacob in the kitchen. No sign of Jacob in the living room, but on the couch was a bearded man. His eyes were zeroed in on his phone, his thumb scrolling. The twins were busy with a pile of blocks.

"Roy, this is Mia Westwood."

He looked up and a smile flickered on to his face. "Nice to meet you. I'm Roy, Annie's husband."

"I know." Mia stopped. What an awkward thing to say. Did it sound as hostile as it felt?

She rushed to add, "It's nice to finally meet you."

That "finally" wasn't necessary. Maybe she should stop talking for the rest of the evening.

Margie appeared, an apron tied around her waist. "Mia, you're here! Wonderful!"

Mia pushed forward an offering: a Tupperware container with a green lid. "I'm sure you already had dessert planned, but I brought some of Eliza's miniature apple pies."

"Yum!"

"I was going to pretend I made them, but I realized no one would eat them then."

Margie laughed. "That isn't true. They look lovely, and they'll be the perfect addition to the homemade vanilla cinnamon ice cream I have planned."

Hank walked into the room with a wave and squatted next to the kids. "That ice cream machine I got for you was a great investment."

A light flicked on in the hallway, and Caroline floated into view. Her voice small, she said, "Hi."

Air flooded Mia's lungs. She realized she was smiling. "Hi, Caroline! How are you enjoying your time on the island?"

"It's lovely here. I don't know how I'll go back."

Mia's blood flashed with heat, in every vein, all at once.

She forced herself to laugh. "I know what you mean."

"I'm about to bring out the appetizers. Everyone can take their seats," Margie said.

Roy stood, eyes still on his phone, and walked to the table. Caroline and Annie stooped to pick up the kids.

"I'll help you, Margie," Mia said firmly.

She stepped into the kitchen. She wasn't going to give Margie the option to deny her.

It was the first decisive thing she'd done, and it felt good – until she walked into Jacob's chest.

"Oh, hey," he said, peering down at her.

Her heart lodged in her throat. His cologne was nice. Subtle. "I'm sorry. I need to look where I'm going."

"That's okay." He shot a glance at Margie. "I wanted to talk to you for a second anyway. Maybe outside, away from the chaos."

"Don't be gone too long!" Margie barked. "I can't promise they'll save you any of the saltfish fritters!"

"We'll be right back." He opened the kitchen door. "After you."

She should've had a snack before she came—her stomach was flipping now.

The sun hit her eyes when she stepped out, the ground shifting beneath her.

Jacob walked alongside the house and down to the water. Mia followed, forcing herself to take deep breaths.

"I figured we would want to be away from prying ears. Plus, the vibe is weird in there."

There were a few white clouds hanging over the rippled sea. A white sailboat floated, empty and still in the distance.

"Yeah, how about that?" Mia glanced up at him, squinting. The urge to faint passed. "Roy seems...interesting."

Jacob clenched his teeth, his jaw tense. "I'm having a hard time not speaking my mind." He paused. "They're trying to make it work, though. I want the best for them. I really do."

Best not to pry. She needed to change the subject. "Baily Jo might have a job for you. If you're not happy at yours."

A smile flickered across his face. "Yeah? That was what I needed to talk to you about, actually. I didn't want to put it in text – it's too crazy to believe. If it hadn't happened to me, I wouldn't believe it."

What was with everyone's paranoia about messaging? "You're really stringing me along here."

He nodded. "I had to make sure I had all my facts straight. It's about Ronan and Quantum Extend."

Her eyes widened. "Oh."

"My boss sent me to deal with a company that handles their servers and data. They fired their last company because they couldn't set up what they needed – a migration of their data and trades on this legacy system. Whatever, it's not important. They couldn't get it to work and couldn't figure out why."

The scene behind him disappeared. He was mesmerizing, talking so quickly, waving his hands. Mia stared.

Jacob went on. "It took some time for me to be sure what I was looking at, but I know why the other company couldn't figure it out. There's nothing there."

She tilted her head. "What do you mean?"

"The AI program Ronan's pushing at everyone, acting like it's a revolution and some amazing investment technology? It's junk. It produces millions and millions of columns of junk. There's no secret to his investing. He didn't invent anything. The most it does it produce a fake monthly investment output for the clients, retroactively claiming to make trades, to make it look legitimate."

Focus. Not on his eyes, on his words.

Mia shook her head. "Wait a minute. What are you saying?"

"Bailey Jo was right. *You* were right. If it weren't such a blatant crime, it would be funny. He's doing exactly what Bernie Madoff did, but using more flowery language and fake technology to hide it. Like Bernie Madoff, Ronan isn't making investments on his investor's behalf. He's not getting amazing returns. I can see exactly how much money they're trading with, and it's not the billions they report."

Mia's hand flew to her mouth. It was starting to click. "You're not serious."

"I am serious. It's a Ponzi scheme, with about twelve hundred people sucked in. He deposits money from new investors into an account, then doles it out to the older investors to make them think he made them a great return. But it's a scam. All of it!"

Mia blinked. "You're sure?"

"I'm sure."

She took a jagged breath and turned to the sea. A man emerged onto the deck of the sailboat, kneeling at a tie off. Mia watched him, her mind turning.

"I have to tell Katie."

"Who's Katie?" Jacob asked.

She turned back. "My friend who's a reporter. Will you talk to her? She can break this story right open. I know she'll be all over it."

"I had a different idea." Jacob stepped closer, his voice low. "What if you're the one to break it?"

She scoffed. "How can I break the story? I'm not a reporter. I wouldn't know where to start."

"Well, fine, talk to Katie, but tell her you want to be a co-author. I'm your source."

Mia shook her head. "That'll turn the whole thing into a joke. 'Actress Cooks Up Wild Financial Tale.' I can see it now."

"You're not a joke," he said softly.

Her breath hung in her throat. There was that cologne again, drifting on the wind.

"Why shouldn't you get credit for this?" he asked. "You're the only one who's been looking at it, the only one who cared. Sure, there's more to learn about being a journalist, but you clearly have the guts for it."

"I don't know." Her stomach roiled again. She turned and looked at the horizon. The sailboat was moving now, slowly making its way out of the bay.

Who was she to report this story? Was she going to go for failed actress *and* failed reporter?

Yet, with Jacob's bright eyes on her, the impossible seemed possible...

"Hey!" a voice called out.

They turned. Caroline stood at the top of the hill. "Margie is getting increasingly flustered that you two are missing appetizers."

Jacob turned back to her. "Think about it, okay?"

Mia nodded, then walked up the hill. Jacob followed.

Twenty-nine

If only they had more time to talk. Jacob didn't care if he got fired at this time – in fact, he welcomed it. People deserved to know the truth about Quantum Extend. Ronan needed to be thrown in jail.

How many people would end up fleeced out of their life savings? Mia had it right all along – Bailey Jo pulling out large sums of money would send the Ponzi scheme crashing down. It was so obvious why they'd gone after her.

Mia *had* to write this story. It was hers to tell, and maybe she'd find her true calling. Just because she was Hollywood royalty didn't mean she had to follow in her parents' footsteps. Just because she was beautiful didn't mean she had to be a movie star.

Not that he could find a way to put that into words.

They got back to the house and took the last two seats at the table. Roy occupied Jacob's regular seat next to Annie, the newly reconciled couple flanking either side of the twins' highchairs.

Annie was in the kitchen, returning with a cup of milk for Noel. She then stooped over Leon to cut toast and blueberries.

Roy sat, stuffing a bread roll into his mouth, steam rising from his bowl.

"I saved appetizers for the two of you, but it wasn't easy," Margie said, laying a plate on the table. "I *finally* conquered the chicken stew I had to throw away last time! And we've got rosemary roasted potatoes with asparagus, cloverleaf rolls, and an apple-cranberry salad."

Roy took a swig of water. "This looks incredible, Margie. Thanks again for having me."

"You are welcome," Margie said, disappearing into the kitchen and returning a moment later with a skillet. "I almost forgot—I made cornbread, too. Half is jalapeno, half is plain for the kids or whoever doesn't like it spicy."

Noel cried out, her fist grabbing at Leon's blueberries.

"Hang on a second," Annie said, "I'll get to yours next, sweetie."

Jacob looked at Roy. His arm was outstretched, cutting a slice of cornbread. He dunked it into his stew. "Delicious."

Jacob clenched his jaw and stood. He cut Noel's toast and blueberries, then cut small bites of cornbread for each of them.

"She's always cranky when she doesn't get her blueberries fast enough," Roy said with his mouth full.

All Jacob could manage to say was, "Yup."

Once the twins were occupied, Jacob filled Annie's bowl with stew, put a roll on her plate, and took his seat.

He filled his own bowl, the steam rising and touching his face, his blood boiling beneath the surface.

The scent of the carrots, potatoes, and chicken in the creamy broth filled his nostrils. He took a deep breath, the heat passing from his face.

"So, Mia," Roy said. "Do you have any movies in the works?"

She shook her head. "Not yet. I'm still figuring out what I want to do next."

Her eyes flicked to Jacob. A small smile formed on her lips.

He smiled back before casting his eyes onto the rolls. He reached for one, even though his mouth was completely dry and the last thing he wanted to deal with was a hunk of bread.

"That's awesome," Roy said. "So many people give up on life. It's inspiring to see someone living out their dream."

"Thanks, I guess?" Mia set her spoon down. "I don't think it's that simple."

"Of course it is," Roy said. "It's not easy, but you need to keep your head clear."

Annie touched his arm. "I think Mia is allowed to have her own opinion about her life."

Roy dabbed at the corner of his mouth with a napkin. "Sure, but so many people sleepwalk through life and accept what's given to them. They're not proactive about getting what they want, and they end up getting what they deserve."

Caroline sat back, her eyebrows scrunched. "What's that supposed to mean?"

"Does anyone need a drink refill?" Margie asked loudly. "I can make lemonade."

"You know, I think I'll get a soda," Hank announced, standing from his seat. "Anyone else?"

"No one is going to build the perfect life for you," Roy said. "You have to do it, and if you don't, you have no one to blame but yourself."

Caroline scoffed. "At the expense of anyone who gets in your way, right?"

He tilted his head. "That's not what I said."

Jacob, better than anyone, knew what was about to happen. Yet he had no urge to stop it. He slowly filled his salad plate, sure to top it with slices of apples.

"You're living it, though," Caroline said with a laugh. "All your talk about positivity and building the life you want. What about the life your kids want? And your wife?"

Jacob looked at Annie. She slowly picked at her roll, her eyes focused on Caroline.

"Okay, Caroline." Roy set his water glass down, a half-smile on his face. "I know you're not in a good place. You're depressed –"

"I'm not depressed," Caroline snapped. "My dad just died. I'm grieving."

"You're depressed," Roy repeated, "and you will be until you learn to take control of your life."

Jacob sat back. He could stop it. He could, but...

Caroline's mouth popped open. "Is that right?"

"Roy, you can't tell people they're depressed!" Annie hissed.

Caroline crossed her arms. "This is so interesting. I've heard about people doing this, but I've never seen it in person."

Roy raised his eyebrows. "Seen what?"

"Someone with their head so far up their –"

Margie cut her off. "Language, Caroline. We've got impressionable ears here!"

Caroline smiled. "I was going to say ego. So far up their own ego they start believing their own narrative. Preaching it, even."

"Yeah, okay," Roy rolled his eyes. "I shouldn't have pointed out the obvious. Don't shoot the messenger because you don't want to hear the truth."

Jacob scanned the table. Mia's eyes were wide, her head volleying back and forth. Annie's expression was blank. Margie's cheeks blazed red. Hank shot Jacob a stern look.

He knew what it meant. *Don't say a word.*

"You wanted to gain control of your life," Caroline continued, "after catching a glimpse of your own mortality. Usually, guys do this around their midlife, so kudos to you. You were early."

"Midlife," Roy sputtered. "I'm not –"

Caroline went on. "Some guys get secret younger girlfriends, others buy impracticable convertibles. You couldn't follow the trend. You had to abandon your family, then tell them it was for their own good."

"I did not abandon my family," Roy said firmly, pointing a finger into the table.

"Then you came back with all this positive self-talk to rationalize dumping all of the work of family life on your wife so you can keep living an exciting, outdoorsy bachelor life."

"Is anyone ready for dessert?" Margie asked in a shaky voice. "It's never too early for dessert."

Roy opened his mouth. "That's – you're not even –"

"So, before you smugly tell me what I need to do with my life," Caroline said, sitting back. "You should put your life in order and face some truths of your own."

"Says the woman who came running back to the ex-husband *she* abandoned," Roy spat out.

Caroline flinched and let out a breath. "It's true. I did come running back. He's been kind to me. I don't deserve it, but at least I can admit that."

Jacob sighed. "Caroline."

"All right, everyone." Annie stood. "I don't like raised voices around the twins. You're welcome to continue this argument outside."

"Well said," Margie added, standing from her seat. "I'm going to bring out dessert now."

She walked to the kitchen, Hank close behind her, his arms stacked with plates.

"Somehow, my appetite is ruined," Roy said, tossing his napkin down. "Let's go, Annie."

He tried to unbuckle Noel from her seat, but she squealed, clutching a fistful of cornbread.

Annie crossed her arms. "I'm going to stay for dessert."

"Whatever. Fine." He rolled his eyes and disappeared through the doorway.

Jacob let out a breath.

Annie stood, staring at the table.

"I'm sorry," Caroline said, her cheeks flushed red. "When he brought up my dad –"

Annie held up a hand. "It's okay." She bit her lip. "I didn't know you felt that way."

"I didn't either."

Mia cleared her throat and set her napkin on the table. "I should go."

He wanted to stop her, but he didn't have the words. Margie pleaded with her in the kitchen, their tones hushed, but soon after, he heard the door open and close.

They sat in the quiet of the twins' babbling. After a few minutes, Annie turned from her little charges.

"Does everyone think I'm an idiot?" Annie asked, her voice small.

"No," Jacob said firmly.

"That's not it at all," Caroline said. "You're incredibly kind, and forgiving, and honest. You're like Jacob. You're too good."

Annie scratched her cheek. Jacob thought she might be wiping a tear. It was too hard to tell.

"I've been frustrated with Roy," Jacob said. "I was sure he'd gotten frightened. Confused."

"Yeah." Annie nodded. "That's what I had hoped, too."

"It's like I don't recognize him now," Jacob said.

"Me either." Annie flopped into her chair. "I'm actually – it's a relief to know I'm not the only one who feels that way."

"Not at all," Caroline said. "It's glaring."

Annie let out a breath. "I kept twisting myself into thinking it was me. It had to be me."

"It's not you," Jacob said.

Margie arrived with bowls of ice cream. Hank carried out a plate stacked with mini apple pies.

"I have a lot to think about," Annie said. "But now, dessert."

"That's the spirit!" Margie said, beaming.

After cleaning up, Caroline and Jacob cleared the table as Annie and Margie got the twins in the car.

Caroline made a face. "I'm sorry I ruined Sunday Dinner."

"You didn't ruin it." He paused. "You made it eventful."

She scoffed. "I'm sorry I dropped in on you like this, too. I know what I'm doing isn't fair. I appreciate you being so kind to me."

Jacob nodded, stacking bowls. "Of course."

She lowered her voice. "I didn't come here with the intent of trying to win you back. I don't know why I came."

He paused and smiled at her. "A random act of Caroline."

"We gave it a good try, didn't we? But it didn't work."

Jacob shook his head. "I always figured it was my fault. I shouldn't have kept asking you to marry me."

"How can you say that?" Caroline shook her head. "I mean, I think Roy is full of it, but he has a point. I need to sit down and figure out what I'm doing with my life. That's how I ended up losing you. I can never face that fear of picking the wrong thing, so I picked nothing. It's no way to live."

He wasn't sure what to say, so he offered her a smile.

She smiled back. "You have a good thing going here. Don't be blind to it."

"Yeah. I love this island."

"Not just this island." She raised her eyebrows. "Your island romance."

He scoffed. "We're friends."

"Yeah, uh huh." She smiled. "I know this is weird coming from me, but don't miss out on your life. Go after it, okay? Go after it with the assurance of a man who found his purpose on the side of a snowy mountain and returned to tell us about it."

Jacob laughed. Margie had gotten to her too, apparently. "Okay. Sure."

Thirty

It took only a few days for Mia and Katie to finish the article on Quantum Extend, then two weeks of rushing to get it published. The editors at the paper couldn't wait to get it out; the lawyers held them up, nervous about the language and claims, but ultimately relented.

Once it was published, the world cracked open. As predicted, investors immediately fled, and Ronan ran out of money to pay them. Previous employees stepped forward and corroborated the story, adding stories of Ronan retaliating and targeting anyone who defied him.

It was more exciting than any film Mia had ever been a part of. More satisfying than any premier, any positive review, and far more important than any silly interview she'd ever given.

Waking up each morning and watching her work and her words spread across the country like wildfire was a thrill. Her spark erupted into other scandals, burning the entire facade down.

The SEC held a press conference, acknowledging the need to investigate the claims against Quantum Extend. They denied comment on their failure to follow up on Mia's initial claims.

Miraculously, within three days of the story breaking, Ronan pulled out of Bailey Jo's lawsuit, and within a week, the prosecutors withdrew their case.

Her first stop when she found out was the tea shop.

"They know they have nothing to go on," Bailey Jo said, beaming.

She came to celebrate, dressed head-to-toe in a hot pink jumpsuit and dragging an enormous gift basket behind her. Inside it were designer leggings, a couture dress, perfumes and piles of skincare products Mia had never heard of but was sure cost more than a month of rent.

"There's no way I could ever really thank you," Bailey Jo said solemnly and loudly over the cellophane wrapped around the basked as she pushed it forward. "But I needed you to know you're amazing."

Mia grinned. "Thank you, Bailey Jo. I can't believe I was able to help. I can't believe what's happening."

Patty tried to lift the basket with one arm and stumbled under its weight. "Would you look at that! We should put this on display somewhere."

"Is there a bunny in there?" Russell asked.

Bailey Jo wagged a finger. "No bunny, Mr. Westwood. It's not Easter."

Ha laughed.

She went on. "Your daughter is a genius, and you should really stop trying to push her to follow in your footsteps. You're holding her back from her true calling: ruining rich men's lives."

He laughed and threw his hands up. "I'm not pushing her! I never push her!"

Sheila *tsk*ed. "That sounded pretty pushy right there."

"You can all relax," Mia said. She couldn't stop smiling. "No one's pushing me. I think it just took me some time to figure out what to do with myself."

Sheila beamed at her. "To find your calling."

"To embrace your gifts," Bailey Jo added.

Mia laughed. "Okay, sure. Thank you, everyone."

The door to the tea shop opened with a jingle and Jacob's voice rang through. "To bring down the smug architect of a huge Ponzi scheme."

Mia spun around. Jacob stood with his tousled hair and gorgeous eyes. In his arms was a white bakery box.

They'd corresponded about the story, of course, but she hadn't seen him since that fateful dinner at Margie's.

"Hi, Jacob." Her voice ran out at the end, slipping into a whisper. She cleared her throat. "It's nice to see you."

"I had to congratulate you on your success." He popped open the box. Inside was an enormous chocolate chip cookie in the shape of a star and the words, "Happy Retirement from Hollywood!" written in pink.

Mia laughed, covering her mouth. "Wow, an impromptu retirement party."

"No," he shook his head. "You're always a star to me. Get it?"

"Why don't we take the basket out on the patio?" Sheila announced. "Russell, can you carry it?"

"If you want me to strain my neck," he said.

Patty gave him a push. "You'll be fine. Lift with your legs, not your neck."

They shuffled away. Silence fell over the tea shop, with only the sound of air pushing out of the vents.

"How did you know I loved that cookie cake so much?" Mia asked.

"I saw your face when I gave it to you." He paused. "I hope this joke isn't offensive."

"Not at all. I feel free. I've never felt so alive."

"I'm glad." He stared at her, his wide smile slowly slipping away.

"Did Caroline make it back to Australia okay?" she asked, avoiding her real question: was he going to join her?

"She did. She felt a lot better after coming here and having a break from her life." A half-smile. "And after telling Roy off. That was a real highlight for her."

Mia laughed. "It was a highlight for all of us. How's Annie doing?"

"She put a pause on Roy moving back in. She's insisting they see a couple's therapist to figure out what they're both thinking."

"Good for her. She deserves the best."

"She does." He set the box on the table. "Caroline wanted me to tell you she had no intention of trying to get back together with me."

Mia's heart leapt. "Oh?"

"She seemed to think you would want to know that." He winced, looking up. "She seemed to think…"

Mia couldn't stop looking into his eyes. She was locked in, her chest burning. "What about true love and all that?"

"I still believe in that. Of course." He took a step closer. "But it was somewhere else all along. With a rising star. A beautiful fireball, sent to Earth to humble us all."

"I don't think fireballs are sent to Earth."

"I don't know much about fireballs," he murmured, getting closer. "But I know a thing or two about what it's like to burn for someone."

The ground shifted beneath her. "I thought…"

He cocked his head to the side. "What?"

A small breath of a laugh escaped her and she looked down, then back at him. "I thought you were in love with Annie, at first. Then Caroline. I never thought…"

He put his hands on her waist and leaned in, touching his forehead to hers. "No, Mia. It was you. Always you."

She closed her eyes, the soft touch of his lips on hers. A burst of energy exploded from her chest and she leaned into him, kissing him back, letting herself fall into his arms.

Epilogue

He'd declined Annie's offer to meet at the house. She had to find a new meeting spot, but the thought of sitting across from him at a restaurant made her stomach turn.

All those people around them, laughing and having a good time, while her life fell apart. What if she burst into tears? What if she had to throw up?

Late at night, when Annie was up with the twins, she could convince herself she could be brave. Talk to him. Tell her what *she* felt, and not in the measured tones she used in couple's therapy, going around and around with him promising to listen.

It was the sunlight which killed her resolve. She sat in the tea shop, across from Mia and Jacob, nearly convinced she should cancel the meeting entirely.

"He probably can't face what he's leaving behind," Jacob said.

He opened his mouth to add something, but stopped when he saw Annie's face.

Annie didn't need to hear the rest of his thought. He was going to say, "Coward."

They were both cowards, in a way.

"I have an idea," Mia said. "Why don't you tell him to come to the tea shop after we close for the day? It'll be all yours. I'll make tea and some sandwiches, then leave you in peace."

Patty popped her head into the room. "Yes! He needs to know you have friends here."

Annie let out a breath. "He knows."

During their last argument, it was something he had bizarrely held against her. He said she was unwilling to move to the mainland because she had "too many other relationships" here.

She wasn't thinking clearly at the time, but it was the people from those "relationships" who had helped her stay afloat when he'd left.

She'd have to remember to say that to him.

"Well, he's going to see it again," Patty said. "You'll meet him here and there's nothing else to discuss."

Annie nodded. She picked up the pink and gold teacup and lifted it to her lips. Black tea always helped settle her stomach. She'd ask Mia to brew that for them again. She would need it.

. . .

That evening, Annie stood outside of the tea shop, wind tearing through her hair, whipping strands in front of her eyes. She could see through the warm glow of the window that Roy was already inside. Clouds swirled above her, dark and all-encompassing.

She took a breath and pushed the door open.

"Hey." Roy walked over when he saw her. "How are you?"

"Good," she said shakily, taking off her coat.

The day had been sun-filled, but Annie couldn't get warm. She couldn't eat much, either, leaving her stomach empty and filled with cotton.

"This place is nice."

Annie nodded. "It is."

"Romantic."

Mia came out of the kitchen with a three-tiered stand filled with sandwiches and treats.

"Shall we?" Roy asked.

"Yeah."

They followed Mia into the London-themed tearoom. She set down the food, and turned to Annie before pulling her in for a hug.

"See you on the other side," she whispered.

Annie smiled. "Thanks."

As Mia disappeared through the front door, they took their seats. Annie's teacup was the pink and gold one again, filled to the brim with tea. Roy's was an empty white cup.

"I'm guessing you've reconsidered my offer," Roy said.

His offer. That she and the twins would keep living on the island, and that Roy would use their family house as his "home base."

But he wouldn't be tied to it. Weekends he might need to go out and adventure. He'd keep his apartment in Seattle for work and other things. They'd be a family – but only on his terms.

It seemed silly now, but at first, Annie was willing to accept this offer. For months, she'd been waiting for Roy to come back, not just to them, but to his senses. The thought of having to share custody of the twins – of not being there every morning they woke up, not having every minute of Christmas with them – it was too much to bear.

It took weeks for her to unwind her thoughts. The problem wasn't accepting less for herself. She could do that, endlessly, if it was better for everyone else.

The problem was accepting less for Leon and Noel. A father who came and went on a whim – or worse, on the impulses of his own weakness. How would the twins feel after a tantrum or a bad day sent their father away for a week? How would she explain that to them?

Once she saw that scene playing out, over and over, she could think of nothing else. Her choice was clear.

"I'm not here to argue," Annie said.

He sighed. "Good, because I don't want to."

"I met with an attorney. I am filing for a divorce."

Roy dropped a cucumber sandwich onto his plate. "What? I thought we were making progress. You said if we took things slow –"

She cut him off. "I wanted to take things slow so I had time to think."

"And this is what you came up with? Giving up on our family because it doesn't fit your idea of what a perfect family is?"

Twisting, twisting, twisting. This was what Roy did. The new Roy, at least.

It was Annie's fault that their family was being torn apart, not his. It was Annie whose expectations of family were too high. It was Annie who needed to compromise.

"I'm not giving up on our family. I'm happy with my family. It happens to be made up of me and the twins. You left it long ago."

He scoffed. "And why did I have to do that, Annie?"

She took a sip of tea. The same blend she'd had earlier, except now she didn't need it to calm her stomach.

There was no nausea. The tears weren't coming. The hands that had been clasped around her neck fell away.

This was the right decision. Finally.

"I don't know why you had to do that, Roy. I only know that you did it, and now I have to figure out what I'm going to do." She set the teacup down. "Being left by you one time was painful enough – for all of us. I'm not going to let you keep doing it."

"You think you're winning by threatening to divorce me?" He threw his hands up. "Fine, I'll get rid of the apartment. Are you happy now?"

"Keep it, Roy. I'm not trying to win. This isn't a negotiation tactic. This is me realizing what *I* need."

He stood, taking the napkin off his lap and throwing it to the floor. "I guess I'll see you in court."

Roy stormed off, the gust of air in his wake lifting her hair.

Annie took a deep breath, then another sip of tea. "See you then, Roy."

That night, for the first time in their lives, both twins slept through the night. Annie did too, and woke with sunlight touching her face.

It was going to be a good day.

The Next Chapter

Introduction to *A Spot of Grace*

Return to San Juan Island in book six of the Spotted Cottage Series! Still reeling from her ongoing divorce, Annie sets her sights on putting her life back together and figuring out single motherhood. The *last* thing on her mind is romance, but when she has to move back in with her mom, she can't help but notice the handsome fireman single dad living across the street...

Reader's Newsletter

Want to dive deeper into the Spotted Cottage Series?

Sign up to Amelia's newsletter and get bonus content from the entire Spotted Cottage series including:

- Rick's postcard to Addy
- Recipes from Eliza and Patty
- A bonus chapter with Sheila and Russell's first Christmas

Visit https://mailchi.mp/0548bfa882d1/rick to get your copy now!

About the Author

Amelia Addler writes always sweet, always swoon-worthy romance stories and believes that everyone deserves their own happily ever after.

Her soulmate is a man who once spent five weeks driving her to work at 4AM after her car broke down (and he didn't complain, not even once). She is lucky enough to be married to that man and they live in Pittsburgh with their little yellow mutt. Visit her website at AmeliaAddler.com or drop her an email at amelia@AmeliaAddler.com.

Also by Amelia...

The Spotted Cottage Series

The Spotted Cottage by the Sea
A Spot of Tea
A Spot at Starlight Beach
Spotted at Lighthouse Bay
A Spot of Summer
A Spot of Grace

The Westcott Bay Series

Saltwater Cove
Saltwater Studios
Saltwater Secrets
Saltwater Crossing
Saltwater Falls
Saltwater Memories
Saltwater Promises

The Orcas Island Series

Sunset Cove
Sunset Secrets
Sunset Tides
Sunset Weddings
Sunset Serenade